George M. Davis, Frank E. Martin

Firebrands

George M. Davis, Frank E. Martin

Firebrands

ISBN/EAN: 9783337363840

Printed in Europe, USA, Canada, Australia, Japan

Cover: Foto ©Andreas Hilbeck / pixelio.de

More available books at **www.hansebooks.com**

Fighting the Fire

FIREBRANDS

3

BY
FRANK E. MARTIN
AND
GEORGE M. DAVIS, M.D.

WITH ILLUSTRATIONS
FROM PHOTOGRAPHS

School Edition

BOSTON
LITTLE, BROWN, AND COMPANY
1912

PREFACE

EVERY year fire destroys an enormous amount of property in the United States. Of this great loss by which our country is made just so much poorer, for property destroyed by fire is gone forever and cannot be replaced, a large proportion is due to carelessness, thoughtlessness, and ignorance. Nor is it a property loss only. Every fire endangers human life, and the number of lives lost in this way in one year is truly appalling.

It has been estimated that if all the buildings burned in one year were placed close together on both sides of a street, they would make an avenue of desolation reaching from Chicago to New York City. At each thousand feet there would be a building from which a severely injured person had been rescued, and every three-quarters of a mile would stand the blackened ruins of a house in which some one had been burned to death.

Children are allowed to burn dry leaves in the fall, and their clothing catches fire from the flames; women pour kerosene on the fire in their kitchen stoves, or cleanse clothing with gasoline near an open blaze; thoughtless men toss lighted cigars and cigarettes into a heap of rubbish, or drop them from an upper window into an awning; the head of a parlor match flies into muslin draperies; a Christmas-tree is set on fire with lighted candles, or a careless hunter starts a forest fire which burns for days and destroys valuable timber lands. There are hundreds of different ways in which fires are set. The majority of these fires, which cause great loss of life and property and untold suffering, are preventable by ordinary precaution.

This little book has been written for the special purpose of teaching children how to avoid setting a fire, how to extinguish one, or how to hold one in check until the arrival of help. Each story tells how a fire was started, how it should have been avoided, and how it was put out: Mr. Brown Rat builds his nest with matches which were left around the house; Careless Joe pours hot ashes into a wooden box; or boys light a bonfire and leave the hot embers, and then old North Wind comes along and has a bonfire himself.

At the end of each lesson there are instructions regarding the fire in question. There are also chapters on such subjects as our loss by forest fires, the work of our firemen, common safeguards against fire, how to act in case the house is on fire, and first aid to those who are injured by fire,—how to treat scalds and burns, how to revive persons who are suffocated by smoke, etc. A thoughtful reading of this book should make the present generation a more careful and less destructive people, and the entire country richer and more prosperous.

CONTENTS

9

LIST OF ILLUSTRATIONS

FIREBRANDS

11

BROWNIE'S MISFORTUNE

POLLY'S cage had just been hung out on the back porch, and she was taking a sun bath. She ruffled up her feathers and spread out her wings and tail.

She knew she was pretty, and as the sun brightened her plumage, she arched her neck, and looked down at herself, saying over and over, "Pretty Polly! Polly! Pretty Polly!"

Then she threw back her head and laughed one of those jolly, contagious chuckles that made everyone laugh with her.

While she sat there, talking and laughing, a big brown rat came creeping up the steps. Polly had often seen him before, for he came to the house every day to find something to eat; and as he always stopped to have a chat, the two had become good friends.

"Good morning, Polly," said Mr. Brown Rat. "You seem very happy this morning."

"Why shouldn't I be happy?" replied Polly. "See how pretty I am. Besides, I have nothing to do all day but sit here and eat crackers and watch the people. By the way, Brownie, run into the house and get me a cracker now."

"I can't get any more crackers, Polly," replied the rat. "The last time I went to the pantry the crackers were in a stone jar that had a heavy cover."

Polly ruffled up her feathers, and spread out her wings so that they would shine in the sun.

"You are very pretty, Polly," said Mr. Brown Rat, "but you haven't such a fine long tail as I have;" and he spread it out on the piazza and twisted his head to look at it.

"Ha, ha! you wait until the cat gets hold of it and it won't be very long," replied Polly. "Why don't you shave off your whiskers, Brownie?"

"I couldn't smell any cheese if I lost my whiskers," said Brownie. "And, besides, they make me look dignified with my family.

"Polly, I am going to build a new house," he added. "I am tired of living in barns and stone walls, and I want my family together where it is warm and comfortable. Do you happen to know where I can find some matches?"

"Why, yes," replied Polly, "my master is very careless with his matches. He leaves them around loose wherever he goes. You see, he doesn't use the matches that have to be struck on a box, and every time he lights his pipe he scratches the matches on anything that is handy. They are snapping and cracking all day long. Sometimes they break off and fly away, all on fire. You can find them almost anywhere in the house. But what do you want to do with matches, Brownie?"

"Well, you see, Polly, the little sticks make a good framework for my house. The wood is good to chew and can be made soft for lining the nest; and the bits of flint in the head of the match are fine for sharpening and filing my teeth."

"You and your family won't be able to file out of the house if you light one of those matches while you are filing your teeth," said Polly, and she gave another of her famous chuckles.

"I'll look out for that," replied Mr. Brown Rat, as he scampered across the piazza.

"Don't you dare to build a nest with matches in my house," Polly screamed after him; but Brownie slipped through a hole in the clapboards under the kitchen window and didn't make any promises.

Polly didn't see her friend again for some time and she began to miss him.

One day she heard her master say, "I wonder what becomes of all my matches?" and this set her to thinking.

She sat still on her perch for a long time, scratching her head with first one foot and then another. "I believe Brownie is really building his nest in this house," she said to herself at last; "and he is using matches, too, after I told him not to."

Then she became very angry. She screamed and bit the bars of her cage with her sharp bill until the cook came out and scolded her for being so cross.

Two or three days later Polly was hanging on the back porch again, and the sun was shining on her feathers. She was spreading out her wings, and cocking her head on one side, when, all of a sudden, she saw a thin curl of blue smoke creeping out between the clapboards.

"Hello! Help! Come in!" she screamed. "Hello! Help! Fire! Fire!"

Some boys who were playing in the street came running up to the house at the cry of fire.

"Get a move on!" cried Polly, dancing about in her cage and trying her best to open the door.

"Where's the fire?" asked one of the boys.

"Get busy!" screamed Polly, as she pulled herself up to the top of the cage.

Just then a wagon came tearing down the street. "Whoa!" cried Polly, and, sure enough, the horses stopped in front of the house.

The driver saw the smoke, and he went to work in a hurry, tearing off the clapboards, and showing the boys where to pour water in between the walls, until the fire was all out.

When the man had gone away, and everything was quiet, Mr. Brown Rat came creeping out of the hole, wet and bedraggled, with his whiskers all burned off.

Polly caught sight of him in a moment. "You rascal," she screamed, "you set that fire. You ought to know better than to build a house with matches."

"I do now, and I'll never do it again, never again," replied Brownie meekly, as he went limping away.

Why did the brown rat come out on the back porch?

How did he build his nest?

Of what material was it constructed?

Why do rats like matches?

Why is it dangerous to leave matches scattered around the house?

That rats and mice are responsible for many fires is no longer doubted. The evidence has been plainly seen. Rats and matches are a dangerous combination. For this reason matches should not be scattered around the house.

In most of the European countries only safety matches can be used; this is one reason for the small number of fires in foreign lands as compared with those in the United States.

"CARELESS JOE"

"I DIDN'T mean to lose my coat, Father. We boys were playing ball, and I threw it down on the ground and forgot all about it until I got home. Then I went back for it and it was gone. Some thief had stolen it, I suppose. I can't help it now, can I?"

"No, Joe, of course you can't," his father answered; "but you are always doing something like this, and I want you to learn to be more careful. It is just the same with your work. Half of it is forgotten, and the other half is not well done. I can't trust you to do anything. You are so forgetful and careless that even your school-mates call you 'Careless Joe.' It is no wonder that your mother and I are discouraged."

Mr. and Mrs. Patten were very fond of Joe, who was their only son, and they did everything they could for his happiness; but the boy had grown so careless and selfish that his father and mother were at their wits' end to know what to do with him.

As for Joe, he was a pleasant-faced, good-hearted, jolly boy; but his parents knew that this one bad habit of carelessness would soon spoil him if it were not corrected. They had done everything they could to help him overcome his fault, but he only seemed to grow more careless every day.

Finally Mr. Patten said to his wife, "Let's send Joe to visit Grandfather Knight. He knows how to manage boys pretty well."

Of course Joe was delighted when he heard of the plan, for who ever saw a boy who didn't like to visit his grandfather?

Mrs. Patten wrote to Grandma Knight about Joe's bad habit, which was giving them so much trouble; and the two old people talked it all over and felt sure that they would know what to do when the time came.

"I'll keep the boy so busy that he won't have any time to forget," said his grandfather. "There is always plenty of work on a farm for a good boy."

"He can help me, too," added Grandma. "I'll pay him with cookies;" and she hurried out to the kitchen to make a big jarful of the round sugar cookies that Joe liked best.

Joe was delighted with everything on the farm, and for several days he did very well.

"He isn't such a bad boy after all," Grandpa told Grandma when Joe had gone upstairs to bed one night.

But the very next morning he gave Joe a bucket of grain to feed the hens, and in the afternoon he found the bucket in the barn, still full of grain. When he spoke to Joe about it, the boy answered carelessly, "Oh, yes, I did forget it; but it won't matter much, will it? Hens can't tell the time of day."

"I suppose not," his grandfather replied; "but I don't believe they like to go hungry any better than you do."

The next night Joe went to the pasture to get the cows, and came home driving nine, when he knew very well that his grandfather had ten. He never noticed the difference until Grandpa spoke to him about it, and then he seemed to care so little that the good old man began to think Joe one of the most careless boys he ever saw.

Two or three days later Mr. Knight went to market, leaving Joe to feed the horses at noon. When he reached home at night, the horses had not been fed, and Joe said he didn't think they would mind going without one dinner.

Grandma Knight heard this remark, and she decided that it was about time for Joe to have a lesson. When the boy came in to supper, feeling very hungry after a good game of ball, there sat his grandmother knitting a stocking.

He glanced around the kitchen in surprise. "My stomach feels pretty empty," he said; "but I don't see anything to eat. Isn't it almost supper-time?"

"Yes, my boy," his grandmother answered, with a twinkle in her eye, "it is supper-time; but I thought you wouldn't mind going without one supper, so I didn't get any to-night."

Joe frowned and hung his head. He knew very well what his grandmother meant, and things went a little better for a day or two; but the boy soon fell back into his old tricks.

Every morning Joe emptied the ashes from the kitchen stove for his grandmother. Grandpa Knight had told him over and over again never to empty them until they were cool, and always to put them in an iron barrel that stood in the shed.

One morning Joe went as usual to empty the ashes, which happened to have a good many live coals in them. The iron barrel was full, but Joe was in a hurry to get away for a game of ball. He couldn't bother to empty the barrel, and he surely couldn't wait for the ashes to cool, so he tipped them into a wooden box, live coals and all, and ran off to his game.

Grandma Knight was making another big batch of cookies, and it was not long before she began to smell smoke. She looked all around the stove, but she couldn't find anything that was burning.

"It must be some paper I threw into the fire," she said to herself, and she went on with her baking.

But the smell of smoke grew stronger and stronger, and when she came out of the pantry to slip the first pan of cookies into the oven, she could see a thin blue haze in the kitchen.

"The house is on fire!" she cried, and she ran down cellar and upstairs as fast as she could go, opening all the doors and looking in all the closets to find out what was burning.

On her way through the hall she caught up a fire-extinguisher; but she couldn't find a sign of the fire anywhere. At last she ran out through the shed to call Grandpa Knight from the barn, and there was the wooden box blazing merrily, and sending little tongues of hot flame across the floor.

It took only a few minutes to put out the fire with the fire-extinguisher which she still held in her hand; but when Grandpa came into the house a few minutes later, there was Grandma Knight sitting beside the kitchen table, holding a pan of black cookies, with tears running down her wrinkled cheeks.

"I never burned a cooky before in all my life," she said, trying to smile through the tears; "but I couldn't let the house burn down!" and then, all trembling with excitement, she told about the fire in the shed, and the box of hot ashes.

When Careless Joe came home to dinner there was a pan of burned cookies beside his plate, and that afternoon he had a talk with his grandfather which he never forgot.

From that day he really did try to overcome his careless, selfish ways, and to be more thoughtful and manly. He had learned that fire is not to be trifled with, and that a boy must always have his mind on his work.

Why was this boy called "Careless Joe"?

In what way was he careless?

What lesson did his grandmother teach him?

What happened which taught him a more serious lesson?

How should ashes be cared for?

What kind of a barrel should they be kept in?

What should be done with rubbish and waste paper?

Ashes should never be kept in wooden barrels or boxes, but in iron barrels or brick bins. There should never be an ash-heap against a fence or near the side of a house. Paper and rubbish should not be mixed with ashes, but kept in a separate barrel.

Cellars and basements should be clean, orderly, and well-lighted. Rubbish is a fire-breeder, and may be the means of destroying your home.

MAY DAY

IT was May Day, and all the children who went to school in the little brick schoolhouse at the foot of the hill were going "Maying."

Every sunny morning in April they had begged their teacher to go with them to the woods to gather flowers; but Miss Heath kept telling them to wait until the days were a little warmer, and the woods less damp.

"By the first of May," she said, "there will be ever so many more flowers. If May Day is bright and sunny we will have no school,—except the school of the woods, no lessons but those the birds and flowers teach us. Wear your oldest clothes, and don't forget your lunches. You will be as hungry as squirrels when you have played out of doors all the morning."

The first morning in May was warm and sunny enough to make everyone long to spend the whole day in the woods.

At half-past eight all the pupils in Miss Heath's school were at the schoolhouse door, eager for the Maying. There were only sixteen of them, and they were of all ages, from five to fourteen, for the little brick schoolhouse was in the country, far away from the graded city schools.

The mothers had not forgotten the lunches, and it was a happy band of boys and girls that set off at nine o'clock for the woods. They climbed the hill and followed a cart-path until they came to a shady hollow where a tiny brook rippled over its stony bed.

"We'll stay here for a little while and watch the birds," said Miss Heath. "Sit down under this pine tree, and keep as still as mice until you have seen five different birds."

22

Joe Thorpe saw the first one,—a robin that came down to the brook for a drink of water. Alice Fletcher caught sight of a black and white warbler that was hopping about in the pine tree, and Grace Atkins pointed out a woodpecker that was rapping on the trunk of an old oak.

A golden oriole flew to the top of a tall elm and called down to them, "Look, look, look! Look up here! Look up here! Look up here!" But the fifth bird was hard to find. They had almost given him up when Miss Heath held up her hand. "Listen!" she whispered, and in a moment a song sparrow that had lighted in a little bush near by sang them his sweetest song,—sang it over and over, with his head held high and his tiny throat swelling with the music.

"There are the five birds," said Miss Heath, when the song sparrow flew away; "now for our flowers!" and she jumped up and led the way across the brook and down a gentle slope toward an old pasture that was half overgrown with underbrush.

"You must notice all the different shades of green in the new leaves on the trees, with the yellows and reds on the bushes," she said, as they stood looking across the pasture. "There are almost as many colors among the trees in the spring as there are in the fall, but they are not so brilliant.

"Now, run and look for flowers," she added, when they had climbed over a stone wall and found a narrow foot-path across the pasture. "I will wait here, under this chestnut tree, and you can come back when you are ready; but if I call, you must come at once. It will be lunch-time almost before you know it."

That old pasture was a splendid place to find spring flowers, and the children scattered in all directions, by twos and threes, peeping under bushes and poking away dead leaves to hunt for sprays of arbutus, or Mayflowers as they always

23

called them.

Grace and Alice found some beautiful clusters of the fragrant pink and white blossoms, but poor little Joe Thorpe didn't have good luck at all, so he wandered off by himself to look for hepaticas.

He found them, too, among the rocks at the farther end of the field, blue ones and white ones, and some that were pink and lavender; and when he had picked a good handful for Miss Heath, he saw some "spring beauties," white blossoms striped with pink that swayed gently on their slender stems.

Just then he heard the call to lunch, and although he hurried back to the big chestnut tree he found all the children there before him, their hands filled with flowers. There were bunches of blue violets and white violets, hepaticas and spring beauties. One girl had found yellow adder's tongues with their spotted leaves, and a boy brought a Jack-in-the-pulpit, standing up stiff and straight to preach its little sermon.

After Miss Heath had admired all the flowers, and had sent three of the boys back to the brook for water, the children opened the baskets and spread their lunch on newspaper tablecloths.

Then what a merry picnic they had! They exchanged cakes and cookies, gingerbread and doughnuts. They shared pickles and apples, and divided turnovers and saucer pies,— and they all picked out the very best of everything for Miss Heath, until she laughingly declared that she couldn't eat another single mouthful.

After lunch they told stories and played games, until, all at once, the teacher noticed that the sun had hidden his face behind a heavy cloud.

"I am afraid it is going to rain," she said; "we must hurry

home."

But even before the children could gather up their baskets and flowers, the big rain-drops began to patter down on their heads.

"I don't care," said little Joe Thorpe. "It is nothing but an April shower."

"April showers bring Mayflowers!" quoted Grace and Alice, and then they held their thumbs together and wished, because they had both said just the same thing at just the same moment.

"They bring wet dresses, too," said Miss Heath, "and not one of us has an umbrella. Let's run over to that little pine grove and play the trees are umbrellas. That's what the birds do when it rains."

The children ran down the narrow path and gathered under the spreading branches of the pines, and the trees held out their arms and tried to keep them dry. But the rain-drops came down faster and faster, and it was not long before the little girls' cotton dresses were wet through.

As soon as the shower was over Miss Heath said, "Now you must run home as fast as you can, and put on dry clothing. I don't want anyone to catch cold when we have had such a happy day together."

So away the children scampered, some in one direction, some in another. At the foot of the hill Alice stopped suddenly and said to Grace, "My mother will not be at home. She was going to the village this afternoon to do some marketing."

"Come to my house," said Grace. "You can put on one of my dresses while yours is getting dry."

When they reached Grace's house her mother was not at

home, either; but Grace found the key to the back door behind the window blind, and the two little girls went into the kitchen.

Then they took off their wet dresses and put on dry ones, and Grace climbed up in a chair to hang Alice's dress on the clothes-bars over the stove.

"It will not dry very fast until we open the dampers and let the fire burn up," she said; so she opened both dampers wide, and then took Alice up to the play-room to see the new doll which her aunt had sent her for a birthday gift. The doll had a whole trunkful of dresses, coats, hats, and shoes, and the two little girls had such a good time trying them on that they forgot all about the kitchen stove.

Suddenly Grace cried, "I can smell smoke, Alice. Something is burning!"

"It must be my dress," exclaimed Alice, jumping up and running down the back stairs.

She opened the kitchen door just in time to see the dress burst into flames. "Oh, what shall we do?" she cried. "My dress is on fire! Put it out! Put it out! Quick! Quick!"

"I can't!" screamed Grace. "Oh, Mother! Mother! Come home! Come home!"

Just then a man, who was driving by with a load of wood, saw the flames through the window and came running in to see what was the matter. He snatched the burning dress from the clothes-bars, threw it into the sink, and pumped water over it to put out the fire.

Then he closed the dampers in the stove, which was now red hot, and opened the windows at the top to let out the smoke; while all the time the two little girls stood in the middle of the floor, sobbing and crying.

"That was a very careless thing to do," said the man, when at last they told him how the dress happened to catch fire. "You should never hang anything over the stove. Tell your mother to take down those clothes-bars this very afternoon, and put them on the other side of the kitchen; and remember never to go out of the room again when you have started up the fire. A red-hot stove will sometimes set wood-work on fire, even if there isn't a cotton dress near by to help it along."

"I don't believe I shall forget it very soon," said Grace, as she lifted the handful of wet black rags out of the sink.

"Nor I," cried Alice. "I am glad Miss Heath told us to wear our old clothes."

"And I am glad that I came along before you set the house on fire," said the man. "Don't ever try to dry wet clothes in a hurry again."

Then he went out and climbed up on his load of wood, muttering to himself, "That's what comes of leaving children alone in the house. They are never satisfied unless they are lighting matches or starting a fire."

Why did Grace hang the dress over the stove?

How did it catch fire?

What material was the dress made of?

Would a woollen dress burn as easily?

Damp clothing, or clothes that have just been ironed, should never be hung over a hot stove, for, as the moisture dries out, the clothes quickly ignite. Clothes-bars or a clothes-line should never be hung over a stove, and a clothes-horse should not be set too near it. Many fires have resulted from an overloaded clothes-horse falling on a hot stove, especially when there was no one in the kitchen to

27

watch it.

Children should never be permitted to open the dampers of a stove, or to have anything whatever to do with the kitchen fire. They should not set a kettle on the stove or take one off, and they should be cautioned against climbing into a chair near the stove, as they might fall and be badly burned.

CAMPING OUT

IT was one of those hot drowsy days in July. School had been closed two weeks, and Dean and Gordon Rand were already wondering how they could ever spend the rest of the long vacation in their little home in the city of Boston.

To be sure there were plenty of books filled with charming stories of brooks and pine woods; but reading only made the boys wish they might go to the real country instead of sitting at home in a hot stuffy house, reading about it in a story-book.

One night the two brothers went as usual to meet their father when he came home from work. His tired face wore a happy smile, and they knew at once that something pleasant had happened.

"What is it, Father? Do tell us!" the boys cried in one voice. Their faces were so eager that it was really hard for Mr. Rand to say, "Wait, my boys, until we reach home. Then your mother can share the good news with us."

Mrs. Rand was looking out of the window as the boys danced up the front walk, each holding one of their father's hands. They pulled him along in their haste to hear the news, and she, too, guessed that something pleasant had happened.

Father said that boys couldn't half enjoy good news with dirty hands and faces, so it was not until soap and water had made them clean and shining that he took from his pocket a letter from good jolly Uncle Joe who lived among the hills of Vermont.

"Here is your news," he said. "I will read aloud the part of the letter that will interest you. Now, listen! Uncle Joe says:

29

'Why not let those boys of yours come up and go camping with me this summer? I am going to pitch my tent in the woods near Silver Lake, and I expect to have good fishing and hunting. Send the youngsters along as soon as they are ready. I will take care of them, and give them a rollicking good time.'"

The boys were so delighted that they could hardly wait for Mother to get their clothes ready, and for Father to write to Uncle Joe and tell him when and where to meet them.

At last the day arrived when they were to take the train for Vermont. Their trunk was carefully packed, and they were as clean and fresh as Mother's loving hands could make them.

It was a long ride, but there was so much to see every minute that the time passed quickly. At noon they opened the box of lunch Mother had put up for them. When they saw the sandwiches and the little cakes and apple turnovers, there was a lump in their throats for a few minutes.

The conductor came along just then, to tell them they were crossing the Connecticut, and in their eagerness to catch their first glimpse of the great river they forgot all about being homesick.

Uncle Joe met them at the station. He gave them each a hearty hand-shake and a big hug. Then he lifted them up on the seat of a wagon, and put their trunk in behind, with ever so many other boxes and bundles.

It was not far to the shore of the little lake. Uncle Joe soon had all the provisions stowed away in a large flat-bottomed boat, and it did not take long to row across to the tents on the opposite side.

Do you suppose a supper ever tasted better to hungry boys than that one of fried trout just caught from the lake, with bread and butter, and fresh berries and cream? Uncle Joe served them generously, too,—just as if he knew all about a boy's appetite!

After supper they were so tired with all the excitement of the day that they were content to sit quietly on the little sandy beach, watching the sunset and the changing colors in the clouds. There were lovely shadows on the purple hills, and dim reflections of the trees and sky in the smooth surface of the lake. How much better it was than all the noise and confusion of the city streets!

It was not long before the boys were sleepy, and Uncle Joe went with them to see that everything was all right in their tent. When they saw the bed they were a little uncertain as to whether they would like it. It was nothing but a great heap of fir-balsam boughs, covered over with two heavy blankets, and it didn't look very comfortable; but when they had tried it a few moments the boys pronounced it the softest, sweetest bed they ever slept in.

Morning found them rested and ready for camp life. Uncle Joe took them out fishing, and let them row the boat home. Then they put on their bathing suits and he gave them a swimming-lesson. After dinner they went for a long walk and he taught them to watch for birds and squirrels.

They had never dreamed that the woods could be half so interesting, or hold so many different things. They enjoyed every minute of the day; and the next day, and the next, it was just the same. They never had to stop and ask, "What shall we do now?" There was always something to do, even before they had time to do it.

They met several other boys, about their own age, who were living in a camp farther up the lake. These boys often joined them in their picnics and excursions, and the time was too short for all they found to do.

But they did one thing that came very near spoiling the fun of that happy vacation in the woods.

One night Uncle Joe stayed out fishing a little later than usual, leaving his nephews alone in the camp. The other boys came down to visit them, and one of them suggested that it would be great fun to build a camp-fire.

Dean, who was always a cautious lad, feared it was not just the right thing to do, without his uncle's permission; but at last he gave in to the other boys.

Broken boughs and bark were quickly piled up, a match was lighted to kindle the fire, and in a few minutes the flames were leaping over the dry wood. The boys were delighted with their bonfire, and they ran here and there among the trees collecting more fuel for the flames.

Suddenly they began to realize that the fire was spreading. It had run along through the dry grass and pine needles, and the wind was blowing it straight toward the woods, where they had had so many good times, and where their friends the birds and squirrels had their homes.

At first the boys thought they could put out the fire with pails of water; but they soon saw that it was beyond their control, and they stood still, too frightened to do anything but scream.

Their cries brought Uncle Joe, and some fishermen from the other camps, to fight the fire, and for more than an hour the men worked valiantly. They chopped off great green branches and beat out the flames, they threw on buckets of sand from the beach, they chopped down trees and made a broad path in front of the fire, and finally they dug a trench to keep it from running along the grass.

At last the fire was declared to be all out; but it was not until the men's hands were blistered, and their faces burned and blackened with the smoke. This was not the worst of it, however, for nearly an acre of valuable timber had been destroyed, and the dead trees held out their stiff leafless branches like ghosts of the beautiful pines and firs that had stood there in the sunshine that very day.

The boys went back to their camps very soberly. How their hearts ached at the mischief they had done! They could think of nothing, talk of nothing, but the fire. Dean and Gordon sobbed themselves to sleep, feeling sure that Uncle Joe would send them both home in the morning.

But the next day good, kind Uncle Joe, whom everyone loved, called the boys around him and gave them a long talk about forest fires.

He told them he hoped this experience would teach them never to build a fire anywhere unless men were near to guard it carefully, and not even then if the grass were very dry, or there was the least breath of wind to carry the flames and sparks.

He explained that thousands of dollars' worth of property might have been destroyed, and possibly lives might have been lost by their carelessness. He told them stories of the terrible forest fires that have raged for days in the timber lands of the Northwest. When at last he asked for their promises, the boys gave them readily, for they had learned how very dangerous a fire can be; and for the rest of that summer, at least, there wasn't another bonfire at Silver Lake.

Why did Dean hesitate to start a fire when his uncle was away?

If the boughs had been green or wet would they have burned as quickly?

Did you ever see a fire in the grass or woods, running along like a race-horse?

How do you think these fires are started?

Why are fires most dangerous in the summer and fall?

Forest fires are started from bonfires, by hunters, campers, fishermen, or lumbermen, or by mischievous and careless persons. Fires should never be started unless the ground is cleared around them, and at a safe distance from any building or woods. They should never be left unguarded.

Forest fires have become so serious that many states have appointed Fire Wardens, whose duty it is to patrol the forests.

Watch towers have been erected, from which observations are taken, and in case of fire, alarm is spread by means of a telephone system.

In some countries avenues, equal in width to the height of the tallest tree, are cut through the forests at intervals of half a mile.

These avenues afford a fire-barrier and standing ground for the firemen to fight the flames.

With the many acres of valuable timber destroyed by fire every year, and the indiscriminate cutting of trees by the lumbermen, our forests are fast disappearing. Children should be encouraged to observe Arbor Day, and to plant trees, so that the custom may become more general, and the forests be renewed.

THELMA'S BIRTHDAY

THELMA was a little Fourth-of-July girl,—at least that was what her father always called her, for her birthday came on the glorious Fourth, the day to which all the children in the United States look forward, just as they do to Thanksgiving and Christmas.

Thelma did not have any brothers or sisters, but she had ever so many friends and playmates; and besides, there was Rover,—the best playmate of all,—good, kind, loving Rover, who followed his little mistress like a shadow all day long.

The Fourth of July was Rover's birthday, too; but he never looked forward to it with the least bit of pleasure. When the horns were tooting, the bells were ringing, and the fire-crackers were snapping, you would always find Rover under Thelma's bed, with his head on his paws, and his eyes shut tight. I believe he would have put cotton in his ears, too, if he had only known that it would help to keep out the dreadful noise.

Of course no one had ever told Rover about the Fourth of July, and he didn't understand at all why bells were rung and cannon were fired, and why everyone was eager to celebrate the day.

But Thelma knew all about it. She was eleven years old, and she had often read the story in her reading-books at school. When her father took her on his knee, and helped her a little now and then with questions, she told just how it happened.

"You see," she said, "when the white men first came to this country they formed thirteen colonies; but they were ruled by the King of England, who often treated them unjustly.

"They bore their troubles patiently for a long time, but finally they were forced to pay such heavy taxes that they rebelled. Then they decided to break away from English rule and be free and independent states.

"Thomas Jefferson wrote a paper declaring their independence, and men from each of the thirteen colonies signed it. This paper was called the 'Declaration of Independence,' and it was read from the balcony of the State House in Philadelphia, before a great crowd of people, on July 4, 1776.

"Bells were rung to spread the good news, and ever since that time the Fourth of July has been celebrated as the birthday of the United States of America."

"And what shall we do this year to celebrate all these birthdays?" her father asked, when Thelma finished her story.

"Let's give a party," replied the little girl, and she jumped up to make out the list of friends she wished to invite.

The Flying Squadron

One morning about a week later Rover waked up very early. He slept at night in his kennel behind the barn, and he always kept one ear open so that he could hear the least little bit of noise. But it was not a little noise that waked him this time.

"Bang, bang! Crack, crack! Toot, toot! Ding, dong!" he heard from every direction.

"Oh dear!" thought Rover, "I wonder if this is the Fourth of July! It can't be a year since I heard that noise before." But he did not have to wonder long. A crowd of boys were coming down the street, blowing horns, drumming on tin pans and firing off torpedoes. They threw a fire-cracker into Rover's yard, and it exploded in front of his kennel.

"That's it," he said to himself, as the smoke drifted away in a little cloud; "it is the Fourth of July, after all."

The minute the cook opened the kitchen door he pattered up the back stairs to spend the day under Thelma's bed. His little mistress went two or three times to coax him to play with her; but he wouldn't even come out to eat his dinner, and when her friends began to arrive for the party she forgot all about him.

It was a beautiful evening, and after supper the children played games on the lawn. It seemed to them that it would never be dark enough for the fireworks.

"I wish the Fourth of July came in December," said one of the boys. "It is always dark by five o'clock when we want to go skating after school."

At last it began to grow dark, and Mr. Ward lighted the Japanese lanterns around the broad piazza, and brought out two big boxes of fireworks.

"You children may sit on the steps where you can't get into any mischief," he said. "I will set off the fireworks on the lawn, and then we will have a feast in the summer-house. I saw a man walking down that way with some ice-cream a little while ago."

But even ice-cream was not so tempting as the fireworks, and for an hour the children sat on the steps, watching the pinwheels and Roman candles and red lights that Mr. Ward set off, with two of the older boys to help him.

"O-o-o-oh!" they cried, every time a sky-rocket went whizzing up over the trees to burst into a hundred shining stars; and "A-a-a-ah!" they shouted, when tiny lights like fireflies went flitting across the lawn.

The last thing of all was a fire-balloon, and Mr. Ward called the children down to the lawn to watch it fill with hot air from the burning candle in its base.

It filled very slowly, and the children were so quiet that Rover came creeping down the stairs to see if the noise were all over for another year.

At last the balloon rose slowly above the children's heads. "There it goes!" they cried. "Watch it, now! Watch it!" and they ran along with it as it sailed across the lawn.

A puff of wind blew it lightly toward the house. Then another breeze caught it and carried it over the roof of the barn.

"Look, look!" the children shouted. "It is going higher. Now it will sail away over the trees."

But suddenly a gust of wind turned the balloon completely over. The tissue paper caught fire from the burning candle, and the blazing mass dropped down behind the barn.

"It will set fire to the summer-house!" shouted Mr. Ward.

"And melt the ice-cream," cried the children, as they followed him across the lawn.

There had been very little rain for a month, and the roof of the summer-house was so dry that it caught fire almost instantly from the blazing paper. Mr. Ward and some of the boys brought pails of water and tried to put out the flames; but the little house and Rover's kennel were burned to the ground, in spite of all their efforts.

When the fire was out and the children had gone home without their ice-cream, Mr. Ward said to his wife, "That is the very last time I shall ever send up a fire-balloon. Fireworks are dangerous enough, but a fire-balloon is worse. I believe the sale of them should be forbidden by law, if men haven't sense enough not to buy them."

But Rover, who was sleeping comfortably on the rug outside Thelma's door, cocked up his ears at the mention of fire-balloons. "They don't make any noise," he said to himself, "and I like this bed much better than the straw in my kennel."

Why do we celebrate the Fourth of July?

What was the Declaration of Independence?

Who wrote it, and who signed it?

What fireworks do you like best?

What fireworks are dangerous?

What is a fire-balloon made of?

Why is it unsafe to send up a fire-balloon?

What is the law concerning the use of fireworks in your state?

Every year the celebration of the Fourth of July costs thousands of dollars in the destruction of property by fire, to say nothing of the loss of life from the accidental or careless discharge of fireworks. One of the causes of fires on this day is the fire-balloons. They are easily swayed by currents of air, and the lighted candles set fire to the tissue paper of which the balloon is made. The blazing paper falls upon the roofs of buildings, frequently causing serious fires.

Almost all fireworks are dangerous play-things, and should be handled with great caution. In many states there are laws regulating the sale and use of fireworks, and all over the country there is now a general movement toward a saner and safer Fourth.

THE "E. V. I. S."

IT was a bright, beautiful afternoon in April. The air was soft and spring-like, and the sky as blue as only April skies can be.

The grass was springing up fresh and green, and the robins and bluebirds were singing joyously.

Elmwood was a pretty little village. Its streets were long and level, and there were so many elms among the shade trees that Elmwood seemed just the right name for it.

The village school had just been dismissed, and the street was full of boys and girls who were hurrying home to their dinner; but over in one corner of the campus a group of boys were talking together earnestly.

"I say, boys, we must do it!" exclaimed the tallest in the group.

"Of course we must," echoed one of the younger boys.

"It will be great fun!" and "Won't we make things look fine!" shouted two of the others. And so they talked on, in eager boyish voices, making plans for the Village Improvement Society which they wished to form.

They had already talked the matter over with their teachers and parents, and everyone encouraged them to go ahead. "We will help and advise you all we can," they said; "and it is just the time of year when there is plenty to do about the town."

That evening the boys held a meeting to elect officers and plan their work. Mr. Ashley, the principal of the school, was invited to come, and promptly at eight o'clock the Elmwood Village Improvement Society was formed. Leon Messenger

41

was chosen president, Archie Hazen was made secretary, and Harold Merrill treasurer.

Each and every one promised to do his part and to work with a will to improve the little village of Elmwood; and, with Mr. Ashley's advice, they planned their work for the summer.

First of all, they decided, the streets must be cleaned. That alone would require a good deal of time.

Then some one proposed raking the yards for three or four poor women. "They can't afford to hire it done. Couldn't we do it for them?" he asked.

"Good work!" responded Mr. Ashley. "Then, boys, see if you can't get permission to tear down and remove some old fences. Their owners would probably make no objection to your doing it, and it would be a great improvement to the village."

There were two triangles of land between cross streets. Here the boys planned to plant cannas and other bulbs, and to keep the grass neatly mowed around the beds.

"We might set out some vines to clamber over the telephone poles," one boy suggested.

"Some of us must go about and get the people to give money to buy waste-barrels," said Archie Hazen. "We must never allow paper, banana and orange peels, or anything of that kind on the streets."

"Better still, we must never throw them there ourselves," added Harold Merrill.

"Those of us who drive cows must look out that they do not feed beside the road," said Leon Messenger; "and we might get our fathers to trim up the trees."

"We must be sure to see some of the town officers about

having no more rubbish dumped over the river-bank," said another.

"We'll have our campus look better than it ever did before," declared one of the little boys; while another added, "We'll have Elmwood the cleanest, prettiest village in all New England."

The boys not only planned,—they worked, and worked with a will. The very next day was Saturday, and every member of the new E. V. I. S. was on hand to do his best.

Never had the streets of Elmwood looked so clean as they did in one week's time. Many a poor woman's yard was carefully raked, and several old fences were removed.

Money for the waste-barrels had been given cheerfully, and all the boys were so eager to keep the streets clean that they would not have thrown a paper bag or a banana-skin in the road any more than they would have thrown it on their mother's carpet.

The raking of so many streets and yards, and the tearing down of fences, made a good deal of rubbish. The boys carted it a little way outside of the village, and left it there to dry, so that they could have a bonfire.

One warm night in May, Leon Messenger called the club together after school. "We can have our bonfire to-night," he said. "There has been no rain for a week and it ought to burn splendidly. Let's all be on hand by eight o'clock."

Shouts of "Sure!" and "Hurrah!" were the answer; and the boys were all on hand in good season that evening.

The fence rails made a fine foundation, and the boys built them up in log-cabin style. Then they threw on old boxes, barrels, and rubbish until they had an enormous pile.

"Now let's finish off with some dry fir boughs," suggested

Harold. "They will send the sparks up like rockets."

When everything was ready, kerosene was poured over the brush, and a lighted match soon set the fire blazing merrily. Then how the boys did shout! They danced around the fire, whooping and singing, and pretending they were Indians having a war-dance.

When at last the fire died down, they found some long sticks and poked the embers to make the sparks fly again, and then they sat down around the glowing ashes and watched the little flames flicker out. Finally they all decided that there could be no danger in leaving their bonfire.

"Well," said Archie Hazen, "there seems to be some fun for the E. V. I. S. after all. Let's give three rousing cheers and then go home to bed."

The three cheers were given with a will. Then the boys bade each other good-night and set off for home.

When everything was quiet and the whole village was asleep, North Wind took his turn at building a fire. He puffed out his cheeks and blew on the red embers until tiny flames came darting out to lick the dry leaves.

He sent merry little breezes to toss the hot sparks into the grass, and when it blazed up, here and there, he blew with all his might and swept the fire across the field.

Just beyond the fence stood an old, tumble-down barn, and it was not long before the fire was raging and roaring its way to the very roof. The blaze lighted the sky and wakened the village folk from their sleep.

Men and boys tumbled out of bed and hurried through the streets with buckets of water. The firemen came out with their hose and ladders; but it was too late,—the old barn was gone.

Fortunately there were no other buildings near by, so little damage was done; but it taught the boys a good lesson. They had a meeting the very next morning, and agreed never to leave a fire again until the last spark was burned out, and never to build another bonfire without first raking the leaves and dry grass carefully away before lighting the fire.

"But it did improve the looks of the village to burn down that old barn," Leon told Archie, when they were walking home from school together. "We really ought to add old North Wind to our list of members of the E. V. I. S."

What was the object of this society?

What was the result of their work?

What was done with the rubbish?

How did the fire get started?

What lesson did it teach?

The burning of dry grass, leaves, and rubbish in bonfires, in the spring or fall, is a common practice. Extreme care should be used that it is done at a safe distance from buildings and woods, and it should be constantly watched, as a breeze may fan the flames and cause the spread of the fire.

FOREST FIRES

THE loss by forest fires in the United States for the month of October, 1910, was about $14,600,000.

Thousands of acres of valuable timber were destroyed, leaving in the place of beautiful green forests nothing but a dreary waste of black stumps and fallen trunks.

This was an unusually heavy loss for a single month; but in the spring and fall of every year, especially in times of drought, fires sometimes rage for days through our splendid forests.

These fires are more frequent and disastrous in Minnesota, Michigan, New York, and eastern Maine; but, in 1910, twenty-eight different states suffered heavy loss among their timber lands.

The causes of these fires are chiefly sparks from engines or sawmills, campfires, burning brush, careless smokers, and lightning. More than two-thirds of the fires are due to thoughtlessness and ignorance, and could be prevented. Even in the case of a fire set by lightning, which seems purely accidental, the fire would not occur if fallen trees and dead underbrush were cleared away, for lightning never ignites green wood.

In one year there were three hundred fires among the Adirondack Mountains of New York, one hundred and twenty-one of which were due to sparks from the engines of passing trains. Eighty-eight were traced to piles of leaves left burning, twenty-nine to camp fires, and six to cigar-stubs and burning tobacco from pipes.

Every fire, when it first starts, is nothing but a little blaze which might easily be extinguished; but as it grows and spreads it quickly gets beyond control, unless there is a force of well-trained men to fight it.

There are three kinds of forest fires,—"top fires," "ground fires," and the fires which burn the whole trees and leave nothing standing but stumps and blackened trunks.

The "top fire" is a fire in the tops of the trees. It is usually caused by a spark from an engine dropping on a dry twig or cone among the upper branches. A light breeze will then blow the fire from one tree to another high up in the air, and after it has swept through the forest and killed the tops, the trees will die. This is the hardest kind of a fire to fight, as it is impossible to reach it. The only thing to do is to cut a lane in the forest too wide for the flames to leap across; but there is not always time for this, as the fire travels rapidly.

The ground fire is not so difficult to cut off, as it spreads through the moss and the decaying vegetable matter among the roots of the trees. A broad furrow of fresh earth, turned up with a plow, or dug up with a spade, will stop the progress of the fire; but this kind of fire is especially treacherous, as it will live for days, or even weeks, smouldering in a slow-burning log or in a bed of closely-packed pine needles, and then burst out with renewed vigor.

As all large fires create air currents, masses of light gas, like large bubbles or balloons, are blown about in the air, ready to burst into flame from even a tiny spark. In this way new and mysterious fires are set, often at some distance from the original fire.

An ordinary forest fire travels slowly unless it is fanned by strong winds or driven by a hurricane. It will burn up-hill much faster than it burns down-hill, as the flames, and the drafts they create, sweep upward.

The noise from one of these great fires is terrifying. The flames roar with a voice like thunder, and the fallen trees crash to the ground, bringing down other trees with them.

Birds and wild animals flee before the fire, hurrying away to a place of safety. They seem to know by instinct which way to go, and deer, bears, coyotes, mountain sheep, and mountain lions will follow along the same trail without fear of each other in their common danger.

Some of our national forests, and some of the tracts of timber land owned by big lumber companies, are guarded by forest rangers and fire patrols, and many fires are put out before they do serious damage, by the quick thought and skilled work of these men and their helpers.

It has been estimated that forest fires in the United States destroy property to the value of $50,000,000 every year. In this way the timber in the country is being rapidly exhausted; and unless something is done to put a stop to this waste and to replenish the supply by planting new forests, there will be little timber left in another fifty years.

It is impossible to realize the extent to which our forests have been destroyed unless one travels through these great barren wastes. To ride in a railway train for hundreds of miles through northern Michigan and Minnesota, seeing nothing but stumps, like tombstones of what were once magnificent trees, and short dead trunks, like sentinels on a battle-field, is a sad and depressing sight.

PINCH AND TEDDY

PINCH was a tiny terrier pup when we first brought him home to live with us. He was a plump, round, little fellow, with long, silvery-gray hair. His ears were so soft and silky that every one admired them, and his eyes were as bright as buttons, when we could get a glimpse of them. But the hair hung over them so long that we did not see them very often.

As he grew older we had him clipped every summer. Then he was much more comfortable; and he looked prettier, too, for his coat was as smooth and shining as a piece of satin. The hair over his eyes was never cut; if it were, he could not see so well. This hair was needed to protect his eyes from the strong sunlight.

Pinch was a very aristocratic little dog. He did not like to play with any one whose manners were not good.

Sometimes a street dog would come up to him, with a friendly air, and say, "Good morning, wouldn't you like to play with me for a while?"

But Pinch always tossed his nose in the air and walked away very proudly, saying, "No, I thank you, not to-day."

This often made the poor street dog feel a little hurt; but he would wag his tail and run away to his old playmates. "Don't ever try to have anything to do with aristocratic Pinch," he would tell them, in dog language. "He feels too fine for us. I shall never give him a chance to snub me again."

Pinch liked the softest cushions to lie on, and the daintiest things to eat. He was very fond of his mistress and liked to have her feed him; but he never liked to eat from a dish. He preferred to have her break his food in tiny pieces and feed it to him from her hand.

He had a little bed of his own on the floor, but he liked the soft down puff on the guest-room bed much better, and he often stole away to take a nap there.

Pinch had one very bad habit. He always barked when any one rang the door-bell, and no one but his master could stop him. His mistress often tried to quiet him; but Pinch would look up at her with merry eyes which seemed to say, "I'm not a bit afraid of you. I know you love me too well to punish me." And he kept right on barking.

He liked to go for a walk with any member of the family, and if he were left at home alone, he would sit down beside the door and cry as if his little doggish heart would break. If his master's automobile stopped in front of the house, he would run out and jump up in the front seat, wagging his little stump of a tail.

"I don't mean to be left at home this time," he seemed to be saying; but he would look anxiously at his mistress until she said, "Yes, Pinch, you may go." Then he would fairly dance up and down in his excitement.

One afternoon Pinch came into the house, sniffing about as usual. Suddenly, to his surprise, he came upon a half-grown kitten curled up comfortably under the kitchen stove. The kitten was fat and black, and he had a pretty pink nose and a long tail with a tiny white tip. Yes, and he had roguish-looking eyes, too.

"Who are you, and what are you doing here?" asked Pinch, bristling up angrily.

"My name is Teddy, and I have come to live in this house," the kitten answered politely.

Pinch looked Teddy over scornfully and was not very

cordial. He walked away muttering to himself, "I do hope that saucy black kitten doesn't expect me to chum with him. I don't see why my mistress wants a kitten anyway. I am pet enough for one family."

Pinch was really jealous of the poor little kitten; but Teddy was so bright and good-natured that he couldn't help playing with him sometimes, especially if no one was there to see him; but he couldn't bear to see his mistress pet the cat.

"Here I am," he would say; "don't talk to that cat. Talk to me."

Then he would chase Teddy all over the house, until at last Teddy would turn and box his ears, and that was the end of the game for that day.

Teddy had a funny little trick of jumping up on the sideboard. Perhaps he liked to look at himself in the mirror. Once, when he was playing with Pinch, he jumped up in such a hurry that he knocked off a glass dish and broke it all to pieces. He was so frightened at the noise that he did not get up there again for a long time; but he did sit on the chairs and tables, and even on the beds and bureaus. In fact, he made himself at home almost anywhere.

He was very playful, too, so his mistress gave him a soft ball and a little woolly chicken. He kept them under the book-case in the library, and whenever he wanted a game of ball he pulled them out and played with them for a while.

Sometimes he played with his own tail, chasing it round and round, and twisting himself up double in his excitement. He played with the curtain tassels, too, and with the corner of the tablecloth; but his mistress always scolded him if she caught him at it.

One evening, just before supper, the whole family was up

stairs, and Pinch and Teddy were having a very lively frolic in the dining-room. Suddenly there was a great crash, and the cat and dog went flying through the hall to hide under the sofa in the parlor.

The cook came running in from the kitchen, and down stairs rushed the whole family to see what was the matter. There was matter enough, you may be sure, for Teddy had jumped at the table, missed his footing, and pulled off the cloth with all the dishes and a lighted lamp.

The lamp broke as it fell to the floor, and the burning oil was already spreading over the carpet.

"Fire! Fire!" cried the excited children.

"Water! Water!" screamed the cook, and she ran back to the kitchen to catch up a pail.

"Don't pour water on that blazing oil," shouted the master of the house. "Bring some flour. Quick!"

The children ran to the pantry, and the cook dipped up big panfuls of flour, which they carried to the dining-room and threw over the fire.

The room was filled with a thick, black smoke, and every one coughed and choked; their eyes began to smart, and tears ran down their cheeks; but they worked bravely, and after a few minutes the last tiny flame was extinguished.

"What a queer way to put out a fire!" said one of the boys, after the excitement was all over. "I thought everyone always used water."

"Not when the fire is caused by burning oil," replied his father. "Water will only spread the oil, and make a bad matter worse. Always remember to use flour or sand to smother the flames, if a lamp explodes or is tipped over."

"There is something else we should remember," added his

wife; "and that is, never to leave a lighted lamp on the table when there is no one in the room."

Pinch and Teddy had something to remember, too. The noise of the falling china and the sight of the blazing oil had sent them scurrying under the couch in the parlor; and although they had many another good frolic, Teddy never jumped up on the table again.

Who was Pinch? Who was Teddy?

Where did Teddy like to sleep?

How did he pull the cloth off the table?

What harm did it do?

Why should a cat never be allowed to jump on a table?

What other animals do you know of that have set fires by accident?

Great care should be taken to prevent children and pet animals from setting fires. Many a cat or dog has tipped over a lamp and set the house on fire.

It is safer to place the lamp on a shelf or bracket. Never set it on a table which is covered with a cloth that hangs over the edge, as the cloth might accidentally be pulled off, bringing the lamp with it.

Hanging lamps should be used with caution, as the heat may melt the solder in the chain, thus weakening the links and allowing the lighted lamp to fall upon the table or floor.

A lantern should always be hung up, especially in the barn or stable. It should never be set on the floor where it could easily be tipped over, or where it might be kicked over by a cow or horse.

THE BUSY BEES

EVERYONE in the neighborhood called the Belchers the "Busy Bees;" in fact, they had been called by this name so long that they had almost forgotten their real name.

When the children went out on the street together, the neighbors would say, "There go the Busy Bees;" and if any one wanted a book from the library, or a spool of thread from the corner store, some one was sure to suggest, "Ask one of the Busy Bees to get it for you."

Father Busy Bee had died several years ago. That meant that Mother Busy Bee and the young Bees must work all the harder to keep their home together.

Beatrice, the oldest daughter, was seventeen years old, and almost ready to graduate from the High School. Bradley was a messenger boy at the telegraph office, Burton worked in a green-house on Saturdays and holidays; and Little Barbara, who was only eight years old, earned a good many pennies by running on errands for the next-door neighbors.

Mother Busy Bee was a good nurse, and whenever she could possibly spare time from her children, she left Beatrice to keep the house while she went to take care of any one who was sick and needed her.

It would be hard to find a busier family anywhere, and as every one of their names began with "B," it was hardly surprising that people called them the "Busy Bees." Perhaps they were all the happier for being so busy, for they had no time for quarreling or getting into mischief; and when they did have a few minutes for play, they thought they were the luckiest children in town, and had the very best time you can imagine.

Of course Mother Busy Bee was always sorry to leave her children at home alone; but Beatrice was getting old enough now to be a pretty good housekeeper, and Bradley was a manly little fellow who liked to take care of his brother and sisters.

One night there was an accident at one of the mills in the town, and several people were injured. Mother Busy Bee was sent for in a hurry, and she put on her hat and coat and got ready to go at once, talking all the time as she flew around the house.

"I may be back in an hour, and I may be gone a week," she said. "Take good care of each other, and be very careful about fire. Don't play with the matches, always set the lamp in the middle of the big table, and never go out of the house without looking to see that the drafts of the stove are all shut tight."

She had said this so many times before that Bradley couldn't help laughing. "Oh, mother!" he exclaimed; "you are always looking for trouble. We are too old to play with matches, and we never have set anything on fire yet."

Just then his mother caught sight of a pile of schoolbooks on the table, and another worry slipped into her mind. "There!" she said, "it is examination week for you and Bee, and I ought not to leave you at all. You need to study every minute."

"Now, Mother," said Beatrice, throwing her arm around Mrs. Busy Bee and running with her to the door, "there are ever so many people in this town who need you more than we do to-night. Run along, dear, and don't worry. We'll get along splendidly. I can get up earlier in the morning and have plenty of time to study after the dishes are done. Barbara will help me, too. She is a big girl now, you know;" and she drew her little sister up beside her to give Mother a good-bye kiss.

So Mrs. Busy Bee hurried down the stairs to the street door, calling back all sorts of instructions, and promising to be home in a day or two at the very most.

But the accident was more serious than she expected, and at the end of a week she was still unable to leave her patient's bedside.

In the meantime Beatrice and Bradley had found plenty of time for study, and had taken all their school examinations. It was a circle of merry faces that gathered around the supper table each night, even if Mother were still away and the house so full of work.

Everything went well until one evening Beatrice discovered that the doughnut jar was empty. She knew how much the boys liked doughnuts for their breakfast, and as she had often seen her mother make them, she felt sure she knew just how it was done.

She set the kettle of fat on the stove, put the lamp on a shelf out of the way, rolled up her sleeves and went to work. But it was not so easy as it had seemed, and before the doughnuts were rolled out and cut into round rings, ready to fry, Beatrice was beginning to wish she hadn't attempted it.

"I never thought cooking could be such hard work," she said with a sigh, as she dropped the first ring into the fat, and waited for it to rise and turn a lovely golden brown. But it didn't rise very quickly, and when it did float leisurely to the surface, it was still white and sticky.

"The fat isn't hot enough, I guess," she said to herself, and taking up the kettle by the handle, she lifted the stove-cover to set the kettle over the coals. But the kettle was not well balanced on its handle, and it tipped a little. Some of the fat spilled over on the hot stove and took fire. The flames spread quickly, and Beatrice's gingham apron blazed up almost instantly.

The poor girl screamed with fright, tearing at her apron to get it off, and rushing to the sitting-room for help.

Bradley looked up and saw her coming. "Stand still! Stand still!" he shouted, and catching a heavy afghan from the couch he threw it over her shoulders, to protect her face from the flames. Then he snatched a rug from the floor and wrapped it tightly around her to smother the fire, which was beginning to burn her woollen dress.

Poor Beatrice was badly burned and terribly frightened. She sobbed and cried, partly with fear, partly with pain, for her hands were blistered, and there were spatters of hot fat on her bare arms; but, fortunately, the fat on the stove had burned itself out without setting fire to the kitchen, and that was something to be very thankful for, at least.

Bradley made his sister as comfortable as he knew how, while Burton ran to ask one of the neighbors what to do for her burns; but when their mother came home the next morning, she found a very sober group of children to greet her. And from that day to this not one of the Busy Bees ever wanted another doughnut for breakfast.

Why were the Belchers called "Busy Bees"?

Why did Beatrice try to fry some doughnuts?

How did she set her apron on fire?

Why did Bradley tell her to stand still?

How did he smother the flames?

What lessons do you learn from this story?

Frying doughnuts, or any other food, in hot fat is always

dangerous, as there are many ways of setting the fat on fire. Only an experienced person should attempt it. The kettle should never be more than two-thirds full of fat. The fat should not be allowed to boil up, nor to bubble over. Never put water into fat, nor drop in anything that has been in water without first wiping or drying it. Water will always make hot fat spatter. Great care should be used in moving the kettle on the stove. Never raise it or move it without using two hands, and two holders, one to lift the handle, the other to steady the side of the kettle.

Do not use water to put out an oil fire, as it causes the fire to spread over a greater surface. Smother the flames with a heavy rug or coat. If a woman's clothing catches fire, she should not run through the house, as running only fans the flames and makes them burn all the faster. She should wrap herself in a rug or heavy mat, or roll on the floor.

THE COUNTY FAIR

"OH, Father, please let me go to the fair! You promised me I could a week ago. All the boys are going, and I just can't give it up. Please let me go!" and Harry was almost in tears over his disappointment.

"I know all about it, Harry," his father answered. "I realize how much you have looked forward to the fair, and I should like to have you go. There is a great deal for a boy to learn at a fair, if he will only keep his eyes open, but you see just how it is. I am in bed with a sprained ankle, and your mother cannot leave the baby. So what are we to do? A boy of ten is too young to go to such a place without some one to look after him."

"Yes, Father; but Roy Bradish is going with two other boys who are twelve or fourteen years old, and they asked me to go with them. They could take care of me as well as not. I'd be good, Father. Please, please let me go!"

Harry begged so hard that at last his father yielded, and gave the boy permission to go with his friends.

"I would rather have you go with an older person," he said; "but there seems to be no one who can take you. Be very careful not to get into mischief. Don't shout, or run about, or do anything to attract attention. A quiet boy who takes care of himself is the boy I like to see."

So, on the day of the fair, a warm sunny day in late September, Harry started off with his three friends. He had a dollar in his pocket for spending-money, and a box under his arm, which was well filled with sandwiches and doughnuts. As he bade good-bye to his father and mother, he promised over and over to be good, and to come home before dark.

It was a long walk to the grounds where the fair was held every year, but the boys trudged along, talking and laughing, and having a good time.

At the entrance-gate Harry spent half of his dollar for a ticket, and it was not long before the other half was gone, for there were many things to tempt money from a boy's pocket. He bought peanuts and pop-corn and a cane for himself, an apple-corer for his mother, and a whet-stone for his father.

The other boys spent their money, too; and then they wandered around in the grounds, going into first one building and then another. There were exhibitions of vegetables and fruit in one building, — great piles of squashes and pumpkins; boxes of onions, turnips, beets, carrots, and parsnips; ears of yellow corn with their husks braided together, and corn-stalks ten or twelve feet tall ranged against the wall.

From Stereograph, Copyright, 1905, by Underwood & Underwood, N. Y.

The horses are led away to a place of safety

The fruit was displayed on long tables in the center of the room,—rosy-cheeked apples, luscious golden pears, velvety peaches, and great clusters of purple grapes. It was enough to make one's mouth water just to look at them.

But the animal-sheds were even more interesting. There were handsome horses,—black, bay, and chestnut. Their coats shone like satin; and when their keepers led them out they arched their necks and pranced about, as if they were trying to say, "Did you ever see a more beautiful creature than I am? Just wait a while, and I will race for you. See all these blue ribbons! I won them by my beauty and my speed."

Then there were the cattle, long rows of them, standing patiently in their narrow stalls; the pigs, little ones and big ones, white ones and black ones; and the sheep with their long coats of warm, soft wool.

After the boys had eaten their lunch they watched the horse-show for a little while, and then there was a free circus which they wanted to see, so it was the middle of the afternoon before they found their way to the poultry show.

Such a noise you never heard in all your life as the one that greeted their ears the moment they stepped inside the door. If you want to hear some queer music, just listen to a poultry band at a county fair,—roosters crowing, hens cackling, ducks quacking, pigeons cooing, and turkeys gobbling.

Harry liked the poultry-show best of all. He had some hens at home which he had raised himself, and he stood for a long time watching a mother hen and her tiny bantam chickens.

"I wish I hadn't spent all my money," he said to himself. "I'd like to buy two or three of those chickens."

"Cock-a-doodle-doo!" said a loud voice in a cage behind him.

Harry turned quickly, and there stood a handsome white rooster, flapping his wings and crowing lustily.

"Cock-a-doodle-doo!" he said again, and he walked back and forth in the narrow cage, strutting proudly, and spreading his wings as if to say, "What do you think of me?"

"Cock-a-doodle-doo! I'd like to buy you, too," said Harry.

"He is a beauty, isn't he, Roy?" he added, turning to speak to his friend. But the boys were gone. He walked the whole length of the building, and they were nowhere to be seen.

"Perhaps they have gone back to the sheep-pens," he said to himself, and he ran across the grounds to look for them.

The judges were awarding prizes for the finest sheep, and the long low building was crowded with people, but there was no sign of Harry's friends.

"Where can they be?" he said, half aloud. "They may have gone over to see the cows milked by machinery. I'll go there next."

Just as he went out of the farther door of the sheep-shed he met two men coming in. One of the men was smoking, and as he entered the shed he threw away the short end of his cigar. It fell in the dry grass near a pile of straw.

In a minute West Wind came scurrying across the field, and it was not long before he found the lighted cigar.

"What are you doing down there in the grass?" said West Wind. "Why don't you burn and have a good smoke by yourself?"

The red tip of the cigar shone brighter at the words. "So I will," it said, and it sent up a thin curl of blue smoke.

"Pouf! pouf!" said West Wind. "Can't you do better than that?"

"Of course I can," and the stub burned still brighter.

"Now I'll show you a good smoke," said West Wind, and he blew some dry grass over the cigar.

The grass blazed up and set fire to the straw, and then there was some smoke, —you may be sure!

West Wind danced over the grass with glee. He whirled round and round, tossing fresh straw to the flames, and blowing up the smoke in soft clouds.

In a little while Harry came back, still hunting for his friends. A puff of smoke caught his eye and he ran to see what was burning. By this time the straw had set fire to the end of the sheep-shed, and the flames were eating their way toward the low roof.

"Fire!" shouted Harry; but the crowd had gone over to see the milking and there was no one in sight.

"Some one will come in a minute," he thought, and he snatched off his coat and beat back the flames as they ran up the dry boards.

"Fire!" he shouted again, at the top of his voice. This time a man who was feeding the lambs heard him and came out with a pail of water; and then it did not take long to put out the fire.

Just as Harry was stamping out the last flickering flames in the burning straw, a policeman came running out. "Here, what are you doing?" he cried.

"Putting out this fire," replied the little boy.

"I suppose you started it, too," said the policeman. "I never saw a boy yet who could keep out of mischief."

Just then the two men came to the door of the sheep-shed. "What is the matter?" they asked.

"This boy says he was putting out a fire, and I think he must have set it," the policeman told them.

"No, sir," said Harry, "I didn't set the straw on fire. It was burning when I came up, and I tried to put it out."

"I was smoking a cigar when I went into the shed," spoke up one of the men, "and I threw it away. It must have set fire to the straw. It was a very careless thing to do, and if it hadn't been for this boy we might have had a terrible fire."

Just then Harry thought of his coat. It was his very best one, and his mother had told him to be careful of it. He held it up and looked at it. One sleeve was scorched, there were two or three holes in the back, and the whole coat was covered with straw and dirt.

By this time a crowd had begun to gather, just as a crowd always gathers around a policeman, and the story had to be told all over again.

"He saved my sheep!" said one of the men.

"And mine, too," added another.

"Let's help him to get a new coat;" and he took off his hat and began to pass it around in the crowd.

Just then a newspaper reporter came up with his camera, and, of course, he wanted to take Harry's picture. When the newspaper was published next day, there was the picture, and the whole story of the ten-year-old boy whose quick thought and quick work had saved the sheep-shed and all the valuable sheep from fire.

What is exhibited at a County Fair?

Why is the fair held in the fall?

What did the boys see at the fair?

What set the grass on fire?

How did Harry put out the fire?

Why is it careless to throw away a lighted cigar?

Lighted cigars thrown carelessly into dry grass or rubbish have caused many fires. Burning tobacco shaken from a pipe is even more dangerous, and a lighted cigarette is still worse, as some brands of cigarettes will burn two or three minutes after they are thrown away. When they are thrown from upper windows, they frequently lodge upon awnings, setting them on fire. Cigarette and cigar stubs in the streets sometimes set fire to women's skirts. Occasionally a man burns his own clothing by putting a lighted pipe in his pocket, or he sets the bed-clothing on fire by smoking in bed.

"LITTLE FAULTS"

JAMIE and his mother were talking together very earnestly. The boy's face looked cross and impatient, while his mother's was sad and serious.

Mrs. Burnham had sent Jamie to the store to buy a yard of muslin and a spool of thread. When he gave her back the change, she counted it, and saw at once that there were three pennies missing.

If this had been the first time that Jamie had brought his mother too little change, she would have thought a mistake had been made at the store, or that he had lost the money.

She would have been glad to believe it now. But after she had questioned him, she felt sure, by looking into his eyes— eyes that did not look back into hers— that the boy whom she loved, and wished to trust, had used the pennies to buy something for himself, and was trying to deceive her.

"Oh, Jamie!" she said, "you don't know how it troubles me to think you would do such a thing;" and her eyes filled with tears as she looked into her son's face.

Jamie really was a little ashamed, but he didn't like to say so. "Oh, Mother, you make such a fuss over nothing!" he answered, turning to look out of the window. "It was only two or three pennies! I don't see why you should feel so badly over such a little thing. What if I did spend them for something else?"

"I know it is a little thing," his mother told him. "It isn't the pennies I care about. I would have given them to you gladly if you had asked for them; but I cannot bear to have you take them and not tell the truth about it.

"It is only a little fault, I know; but little faults grow into big ones, just as little boys grow into big men. You must look out for your little faults now, Jamie, or you will have big ones when you are a man. A boy ten years old should know the difference between right and wrong."

Jamie did not seem as sorry as his mother wished he were. "You needn't worry about me," he said, "I'm not going to get into any trouble;" and he put on his cap and went out to join his playmates.

A few days later Mrs. Burnham saw him on the street with a crowd of boys who were snow-balling the passers-by. When he came home that night, she said, "I wish you would not play with those boys. They are rough and rude, and I don't like them. They are not the kind of friends I want you to choose."

This time Jamie was decidedly cross. "Why do you find fault with every little thing?" he asked. "Can't you trust me to take care of myself?"

"I am trying to teach you how to do it," his mother replied; "and I want you to help me."

But this lesson seemed to be a hard one for the boy to learn. It was not many days before his teacher saw him copying an example from the paper of a boy who sat in front of him in school.

"What are you doing, James Burnham?" Miss Jackson asked quickly. "I want you to do those examples yourself, not copy them from some one else. Bring your paper here at once. I am sorry I cannot trust you."

Jamie put the paper on the teacher's desk, and as he did so he said, "I know how to do the examples. I don't see why you should care about such a little thing as that."

"Perhaps it may seem only a little thing to you," replied Miss

Jackson; "but unless you are an honest boy you will never be an honest man. Try to do just what is right every day, or you will get into serious trouble before you know it."

Five or six years later Miss Jackson was visiting an Industrial School for boys, when suddenly she caught sight of a familiar face.

"Who is that?" she asked the superintendent who was conducting her over the buildings, and she pointed to a boy who was working at a carpenter's bench.

"His name is James Burnham," replied the superintendent. "He has been here two or three years, but we are going to send him home next month. He is a pretty good boy now."

"He used to go to school to me," said Miss Jackson. "I think he meant well, but he was careless about little things, and didn't always choose the right friends."

The horses gallop madly down the street

"That was just the trouble," Mr. Bruce told her. "He got into the company of some bad boys, and they led him into all kinds of mischief. At last they began setting fires to some of the old barns in the town; but one night there was a high wind that blew the sparks to a house near by, and it was burned to the ground. Then the police caught the boys, and they were all sent away to schools like this. It has been a good lesson for James, and his mother is proud of his improvement."

"Boys don't realize what a dangerous thing fire is," said Miss Jackson, as she turned to go home. "If they only knew how much property is destroyed by fire every year, a large part of it through carelessness, they would be more thoughtful about starting a tiny blaze that might so easily become a great conflagration."

What were Jamie's "little faults"?

Into what trouble did they lead him?

Why did the boys set fire to the old barns?

Why is it dangerous to burn any building, no matter how old or useless it is?

Did you ever see a big fire in the country? In the city?

Describe it. What damage did it do? How was it extinguished?

Have you read in the newspaper about any big fires recently?

Where were they, and how were they caused?

Was your own house ever on fire? What did you do?

It is against the law to burn a building, even if it is nothing but an old barn. No one can tell where a fire will end if it once gets a good start. Sparks will fly in all directions, and if there is a high wind they will blow for a long distance and set fire to the roofs of other buildings.

A man who willfully sets fire to his own property, or that of his neighbors, is liable to imprisonment. Arson is a serious crime and calls for severe punishment.

TEN YOUNG RATS

Mr. and Mrs. Rat had ten babies. They were fat, glossy, little fellows, with long tails and shining black eyes, and they lived in a snug nest in the attic.

You can't imagine how hard it was for their father and mother to find names for so many children. Mrs. Rat wanted this name; Mr. Rat preferred that; but they couldn't agree on a single one. At last they decided to wait until the babies were grown up, then they could tell just what name would suit each one best.

It does not take long for baby rats to grow up, and in two or three weeks Father and Mother Rat began to name their children.

The biggest one was Jumbo, the smallest they called Tiny. One had a very long tail and he was called Long Tail; another had almost no tail at all, so he was named Bobby.

One rat was named Whiskers, because he had such handsome whiskers, and Spot had a tiny white spot over one of his eyes. Then there were Frisky, and Squeaker, and Listen, and Duncie.

Mother Rat didn't like Duncie's name at all; but he was so very, very slow and stupid that Father Rat wouldn't let her call him anything else.

"We can't expect every one of our ten children to be smart," he said. "If he is a dunce we must call him a dunce. That's all there is to it."

Of course all these brothers and sisters had very jolly times together. They played tag, and hide-and-seek, and blind-man's buff, and all sorts of good games; but sometimes they had dreadful quarrels. In such a large family there are bound to be quarrels once in a while.

When they began to scratch and bite, Father Rat gave them all a good spanking and sent them to bed. Then Mother Rat crept up to tuck them in, with a big piece of cheese hidden under her apron.

The children usually obeyed their father and mother, and tried to be good little rats; but like all boys and girls they sometimes thought they knew more than their parents. Then they got into trouble.

Father Rat had built his nest in the attic of an old-fashioned farmhouse out in the country.

Mr. and Mrs. Barnes, who lived in the house, didn't seem to know anything about the ten young rats in the attic. Perhaps it was because they were very old and deaf, and didn't hear the little feet pattering across the floors and scampering up and down the walls.

But the ten young rats knew all about Mr. and Mrs. Barnes. They knew where Mrs. Barnes kept her cheeses and cookies, and they gnawed big holes and made good roads through the walls from the attic to the pantry and cellar.

They could find their way to the barn, too, where Mr. Barnes kept his corn and oats; and sometimes they used to slip into his hen-house and steal an egg for their supper.

Mr. and Mrs. Rat were very thoughtful about teaching their children. Every morning there was a long lesson in the schoolroom corner of the attic. The ten young rats sat up straight in a row and did just as they were told.

"Sniff!" said their mother, and they sniffed their little noses this way and that to see if they could smell a cat.

"Listen!" said their father, and they cocked their little heads on one side, and pricked up their ears to hear the tiniest scratch he could make.

"Scamper!" and they ran across the floor and slipped into a hole as quick as a wink.

They were taught to steal eggs, and to avoid traps, and when they had a lesson in apples you should have seen them work! Every one of them, except Duncie, of course, could gnaw into an apple and pick out the seeds before Mother Rat could count ten.

In Mrs. Barnes' storeroom there were long rows of tumblers filled with jelly. The tumblers were all sealed with paraffine, but the rats soon learned how to gnaw it off, and then what a feast they had!

They were growing so bold that Father Rat began to be anxious about them. "You children ought to be a little more careful," he said. "You'll get into trouble some day."

"We never have been caught," said Squeaker.

"No," said Frisky, "and we never will be. We know too much for that."

One morning Father and Mother Rat went to visit an old uncle who lived down beside the pond, and they left the ten young rats all alone.

The minute they were gone Long Tail whispered, "Come on, Ratsies; let's go down to the cellar for some jelly."

"Father told us not to," answered Whiskers.

"'Fraid cat, 'fraid cat!" cried Frisky. "Who's going to be a 'fraid cat?"

"Not I," said Spottie. "Not I," said Bobby; and in two seconds they were every one scampering down to the storeroom.

They nibbled away at the jelly for a little while, but Bobby soon found a stone jar with a cover on it.

"Come over here, Ratsies," he called.

Whiskers sniffed at the cover three times. "There are grape preserves in that jar," he said at last.

"We must have some," cried Bobby.

"Yes, yes," squeaked Tiny; "there's nothing I like half so well as grape preserves."

"I am the biggest," said Jumbo, "so I ought to get off the cover." He pulled and pushed, and worked away until the cover came off.

"Goody, goody, goody!" squealed all the rats together, and they plunged in their paws and gobbled up the grapes so fast that their faces were soon purple and sticky with the sweet preserve.

They were not very quiet about it, either. They forgot there was some one else in the house.

Suddenly Listen pricked up his ears. "Ratsies," he whispered, "I hear a noise."

And, sure enough, he did hear a noise; for down the cellar stairs came Nig, the big black cat.

Then how those rats did scamper! They ran this way and that, across the floor, and up the wall, and under boxes and barrels. It seemed to Nig as if the cellar were full of rats. She caught one for her dinner. It was Duncie, of course; and then there were only nine rats in the family.

They were all more careful for a little while; but young rats are very venturesome, and it wasn't many days before they wanted to go down into the pantry.

Listen said he hadn't heard a sound all the morning, and so

they decided to creep down very quietly.

The truth was that Mr. and Mrs. Barnes had gone away for a month, and the house was empty; but of course the rats didn't know anything about that.

There wasn't a single crumb on the pantry shelves, so they crept into the kitchen. Whiskers gave a long sniff, and before the others knew what he was doing, he was up on a shelf behind the stove.

"Come on, brothers and sisters," he squealed. "Here is something that smells good. It seems to be on the end of little sticks, but we can gnaw it off."

"Of course we can," cried Jumbo. "Let's all get to work." He tossed the matches around on the shelf, and the nine rats went to work with a will.

Suddenly there was a hot little flame. Spot's eye-teeth were very sharp, and he had lighted the phosphorus on the end of his match. The flame lighted another match, and a little fire was soon burning merrily.

It happened that Mr. Barnes had left a pile of old papers on the shelf beside the matches. They quickly took fire, and the frightened rat children fled in terror to the attic.

"Oh, Mother! Oh, Father!" they screamed, "something dreadful has happened in the kitchen!"

"There was a bright light, and a queer smell that choked us," panted Whiskers.

Father Rat understood at once that there was a fire. He scolded the nine young rats for being in the kitchen at all. "We are in great danger," he said. "We must give up this home, and try to save our lives. I can smell the smoke now. Hurry, children, hurry!"

Luckily rats don't have to pack up their clothes or throw

their furniture out of the window. They escaped with their lives; but the old farmhouse was burned to the ground, all because Mr. Barnes had left the matches on the shelf beside the papers.

Where did Father Rat build his nest?

Why do rats prefer such places for their home?

What food did the young rats find in the storeroom?

What did they find in the kitchen?

What did they do with the matches?

What happened? Why?

How should this fire have been avoided?

Rats and mice are attracted to places where they can obtain food, such as barns where grain is kept, rooms where food is stored or where refuse is thrown. Buildings, so far as possible, should be made "rat-proof." To insure safety, matches should be kept in tin cans, metal boxes, or jars.

HOW NOT TO HAVE FIRES

I

WHEN a boy plays with matches, or a man carelessly throws away a lighted cigar, he does not stop to think that the fire he causes goes to make up a part of the tremendous fire loss in our country.

This loss amounts to about $250,000,000 a year. Sometimes, if there is a big fire in one of our large cities, the sum is much greater; sometimes it is a little less.

This average loss of $250,000,000 means that property is burned up at the rate of $500 a minute for every one of the sixty minutes in every one of the twenty-four hours in all the three hundred and sixty-five days in the year. If this seems impossible to you, just multiply $500 by 60 × 24 × 365.

It is said that two-thirds of all the fires in the country are caused by carelessness, ignorance, or lack of proper precaution, and that they might have been prevented. The question before every one in the United States—men, women, and children—is how not to have so many fires,—because the fires destroy forests which require at least fifty years to grow, timber which comes from these slow-growing forests, houses which have been built at great cost of time, labor, and money, and treasures and heirlooms which can never be replaced.

Besides this loss of property there is also a great loss of life, which is too appalling to consider in this little book.

The very best way not to have fires is not to set them. If you stop to think of it, there are not so very many different things that will start fires. Matches, kerosene, gas, gasoline, hot sparks, burning tobacco, fires in stoves, furnaces, and fire-places, hot ashes, lightning, and fires which start themselves by "spontaneous combustion," are the common causes of our losses; but there are hundreds, almost thousands, of different ways in which fires are set with these few materials.

Matches are one of the most useful things in the house, and also one of the most dangerous. They should be kept in a covered dish, out of the reach of children; and they should never be left lying around loose. The parlor match is especially dangerous as the head often flies off into curtains or clothing. After a match is once lighted it should never be thrown down carelessly. Put the stick that is left in the stove or in a match receiver. Never throw it in a basket of waste paper or on the floor. Even if it is thrown on the ground it might set fire to dry grass or leaves.

You start a fire when you light a match. See that you put it out.

Kerosene, used in lamps, lanterns, and oil-stoves, has caused untold loss and suffering. Never fill a lamp, lantern, or oil-stove when it is lighted. Never use kerosene to start the fire in the kitchen range. Never leave a lamp burning when you go out of the room, as it may explode or fill the house with smoke. Keep your lamps clean and see that the wick fits the burner. A clean, well-kept lamp will not explode.

Never set a lamp on the table so that it can be easily tipped over, or on a sewing-machine where it can be pushed off with the work. Turn the wick down half-way before blowing out the lamp, and when the lamp is not lighted keep the wick below the burner so that the oil will not be drawn up and spread over the outside of the lamp. Never carry a lighted lamp into a closet where clothing is hanging. An electric flash-light is the only thing which can be used for this purpose with safety.

Gasoline is sometimes used in the house for cleaning clothing, curtains, gloves, etc. There is no material in the world so dangerous to handle, except possibly dynamite. Gasoline gives off a large volume of vapor which is both inflammable and explosive. For this reason it should never be used in a room where there is a candle, a lamp, a lighted cigar, or where there is a fire in the stove. The only safe place to use gasoline is out of doors, and even then the greatest caution should be taken. Keep the doors and windows closed so that none of the vapor can get into the house, and be very careful not to let any one come near you with a lighted cigar or pipe. Throw the waste gasoline on the ground; never pour it in the sink or down a waste pipe.

Gasoline, naphtha, and benzine are similar substances, and are equally explosive and dangerous. All cans containing either one should be plainly marked to avoid mistakes, and should not be kept in or near the building. Many cleaning and polishing compounds contain naphtha, and should therefore be handled with extreme caution.

Never leave any of these cans uncovered. Beware of leaks in the cans, and never forget that you are handling a dangerous material.

Hot ashes cause many fires. They should never be thrown into a wooden box or barrel, or piled up against the house, barn, or fence. Put them in a metal barrel with a metal cover. Do not put waste paper, rags, or rubbish in the ash barrel. Ashes will sometimes take fire of themselves, by spontaneous combustion, if they are wet. This is why it is unsafe to leave an ash pile near a fence or building.

Waste papers, rubbish, greasy cloths, oily waste and rags should be destroyed. They should never be allowed to collect in cellars, attics, or closets, under the stairs or in the yard. Keep the whole house clean. Dust, dirt, and rubbish are fire-breeders. This is especially true in factories, shops, fruit and grocery stores, schoolhouses, churches, and all public buildings. It is cheaper to throw away barrels, boxes, papers, sawdust, painter's cloths, old rags—waste of any kind—than to burn it up by setting the house on fire.

THE KITCHEN FIRE

TOMMY TAYLOR was a lazy boy,—there wasn't a doubt of it. He didn't like to get up in the morning, and he didn't like to go to school. When his mother asked him to bring in some wood, he always said, "Can't you wait a minute?" and if she wanted him to do an errand he would answer, "Oh dear! Must I do it now?"

He liked to play ball, of course; and he would spend the whole afternoon building a snow fort or carrying pails of water to make a hill icy for coasting; but he didn't call that work. It was play, and Tommy wasn't one bit lazy about playing.

One noon when Tommy and his sister were eating dinner their mother said, "I'm going shopping this afternoon, and I may not get home until half-past five. I want both of you children to come straight home from school, and at five o'clock you can build the kitchen fire and put the tea-kettle on the stove. If you have a good fire it will not take me long to get supper ready.

"Alice may take the key because she is older and more careful. She may build the fire, too; but you, Tommy, must get the wood, and help her all you can."

Alice was only twelve years old, two years older than Tommy, but she felt very much grown up as she started off for school with the key of the back door in her pocket.

"Wait for me to-night at the schoolyard gate," she told her brother, as they separated at the door to go to their class-rooms.

"All right," said Tommy, "I will wait for you." But he forgot his promise when Jack Marsh whispered to him that the boys were going to build a snow fort in his yard; and he went whooping off with them the minute school was over, eager for the fun of a snow fight.

It was nearly five o'clock when he remembered that his mother had told him to go straight home from school, but he stopped for just one more snowball battle, and when he finally reached home he found Alice at the door watching for him.

"Here, Tommy," she said, "take this basket and get me some chips in the wood-shed. There are enough big sticks for the fire; but you forgot to bring in the kindling this noon."

"I didn't have time," said Tommy, hurrying off with the basket; "but I'll get you some good chips in a minute."

When he began to pick up the chips, he found that they were all wet with snow, for the last time it stormed he had left the door open and the snow had blown in on the woodpile. There were some dry chips in a farther corner, but it was too much work to climb over the wood to get them, and besides, Alice was in a hurry; so he picked up the wet chips, shook off the snow, and carried the basketful into the kitchen.

"I don't believe I can build the fire with this kind of kindling," said Alice, as she began laying it in the stove. "It is so wet that it will not burn."

"Oh, yes, it will, if you use paper enough," her brother told her, and when Alice struck a match and lighted the fire it went roaring up the chimney.

"I knew those chips would burn," said Tommy. "Now put in some big sticks of wood."

Just then the fire stopped roaring, and when Alice lifted the cover to find out what was the matter, she could see nothing but a thin curl of smoke.

"Put in some more paper," her brother advised, "you didn't have enough before."

So Alice put in more paper and chips, and lighted the fire again. It burned up brightly for a minute and then settled down into a discouraging smoulder.

"Oh dear!" she sighed, as she took off the cover and looked into the stove once more, "there is nothing but a tiny blaze down in one corner. Run and get some dry chips, Tommy. I can't do anything with these wet ones."

"I'll tell you what to do," said her brother, who was putting on his slippers and didn't want to go out to the shed again; "pour in some kerosene. That will make the fire burn. I saw Mother do it once when she was in a hurry."

"That's so," said Alice. "I didn't think of that," and she went to the closet to get the kerosene can. It was so light when she lifted it that she thought it must be empty; but when she shook it she found there was a very little oil in the bottom of the can.

"Here, I'll pour it on for you," said Tommy, and as Alice raised the cover of the stove, he tipped up the can and poured a tiny stream of oil over the wet wood.

The little blaze in the corner was still flickering feebly. It saw the oil coming and rushed up to meet it. "Whee-ee-ee!" it cried, "there's something that will burn. That's just what I like;" and it ran merrily across the wood and flashed up to the can in Tommy's hand.

Tommy was so frightened that he let the can fall on the floor, but not before the oil in it had caught fire. Fortunately there were only a few drops left, so the can did not explode; but the wood and paper in the stove were now burning furiously. There was a terrible roaring in the chimney, and clouds of black smoke poured out into the room.

"Oh, Tommy," screamed Alice, "what shall we do? We have set the house on fire!"

"No, we haven't," replied her brother; "it is dying down a little now. Open the windows and let out some of this smoke."

Alice opened the windows, and when the roaring had ceased, and the chips had burned to ashes, the two children sat down and looked at each other. Neither one could speak a word.

Mrs. Taylor came in just then, and when Alice saw her she burst into tears.

"What is the matter?" questioned her mother, sitting down and taking the child in her arms; but Alice could only sob that they almost set the house on fire.

"It was all my fault," spoke up Tommy. "I got some wet chips to build the fire, because I was too lazy to climb over the woodpile and get some dry ones. Then when they wouldn't burn I told Alice to pour on kerosene."

Mrs. Taylor put her arm around Tommy and drew him to her side. "My son," she said, "it was your fault that the chips were wet; but it was ten times my fault that you poured kerosene on the fire. If it has taught you a lesson, it has taught me one, too. I shall never use kerosene again to light a fire. It is a very dangerous thing to do.

"We often read in the paper of serious fires that have been caused in just such a way, sometimes even with a loss of life. Promise me now that you will never pour another drop of kerosene into the stove as long as you live, and I will give you my promise, too. Now let's all build the fire, together."

So Tommy ran cheerfully out to the shed and brought in a big basketful of dry chips, Alice crumpled up the paper, her mother lighted the match, and in a few minutes the kitchen fire was blazing merrily.

Why did Tommy bring in the wet chips?

Why did not the fire burn well at first?

What did Tommy suggest using? Why? What happened?

What might have happened if the kerosene can had been full?

What is the proper use of kerosene?

RULES FOR THE USE OF KEROSENE

Always keep kerosene in a metal can.

Always keep the can tightly closed, and keep it as far from the stove as possible.

Never use kerosene to light a fire.

Never, never use it to start up a slow fire.

You will probably set yourself or the house on fire if you do.

Fill all the lamps and oil-stoves by daylight. If you must fill them after dark, never do so while they are still lighted. The flame in the lamp might set fire to the kerosene vapor in the air, and this in turn ignite the oil. If the fire runs up the stream of oil into the can, the can will explode.

Remember that the three most dangerous things in the world for setting fires are *kerosene, gasoline,* and *matches.*

HOW NOT TO HAVE FIRES

II

THERE is an old saying that "A fool can build a fire, but it takes a wise man to keep it burning." This is not true of the fire in the kitchen stove, which should always be built by a wise and thoughtful person. The kitchen fire has caused the loss of many lives and an enormous amount of property.

In laying the fire use paper and dry kindlings. Never pour on kerosene. Do not fill the stove too full of paper, as the smoke may accumulate and blow open the door, thus scattering the burning embers around the room.

After the fire is burning well, close the drafts. Do not allow the stove to get red-hot, as it will not only warp the covers and crack the stove, but it may set fire to the woodwork on the walls or floor.

A roaring fire will sometimes set fire to the soot in the chimney, or carry burning sparks to the roof of the house.

The stove should be set at least eighteen inches away from the woodwork, and the floor beneath it should be covered with brick, tiles, or a sheet of metal.

Never leave the house, or go to bed, when the drafts of the stove or furnace are open. Overheated furnaces have caused many serious fires in the night. Even a low fire will sometimes burn up unexpectedly, especially if the wind blows hard enough to create a strong draft. Do not allow waste or rubbish to collect near the furnace, and do not keep the wood-box near the stove.

Chimneys should be carefully inspected, and repaired when it is necessary, as they frequently crack with the settling of the house. They should be cleaned occasionally to prevent the accumulation of soot, which will burn with a fierce heat, setting the attic or roof on fire.

If there are open chimney-holes in any of the rooms in the house do not stuff them, or cover them, with paper, especially if they are in the same flues which are used for stoves, furnaces, or fire-places. Chimney-holes should always be covered with a tightly-fitted cap or "thimble" made of metal. These caps can be bought of a tin-smith for a small sum.

If the soot in the chimney is on fire, shake on salt or sulphur to extinguish the flames.

Fire-places add a great deal to the attractiveness of a house, but they are especially dangerous if there are children in the family. The sparks often fly out into the room, setting fire to rugs or clothing; babies crawl too near the open blaze; or little girls stand too near the hearth and their thin dresses or aprons are drawn into the fire by the strong upward draft.

Every fire-place should have a hearth of bricks or tiles at least two feet wide, and the fire should be protected by a wire screen. If there are young children in the household, there should also be a fender to keep them at a safe distance from the flames. Some kinds of light wood, especially chestnut and hemlock, will snap and produce many sparks. These sparks fly out in all directions unless the fire is covered with a wire screen. Do not build a roaring fire in the fire-place, as it may carry sparks to the roof.

All fire-places, open grates, and gas-logs should be surrounded by bricks or tiles, so that the woodwork will not catch fire. In many cities there are laws regulating the construction of chimneys and fire-places.

Pipes, cigars, and *cigarettes* have caused nearly $10,000,000 worth of damage by fire. Lighted matches thrown away by careless smokers have added $15,000,000 more to this enormous waste. Every one of these fires was absolutely unnecessary. Cigar and cigarette stubs should not be thrown into waste baskets, rubbish heaps, dry grass or leaves. They should never be dropped from the window, as they might set fire to an awning, and they should not be allowed to fall through a grating where there may be a collection of waste paper and rubbish. If you see a lighted cigar or cigarette stub in the street, crush it under your heel until the fire is all out. If there is one in your house, throw it in the stove. In this way you may save property and human life.

Christmas and *Fourth of July* are the two happiest days in the whole year for children, yet oftentimes they are followed by sorrow and suffering.

Christmas trees, when they are lighted by candles, are easily set on fire, as they are often decorated with festoons of paper, and cotton "frost," which comes in contact with the tiny flames. Many of the ornaments on the tree are made of celluloid. These ornaments catch fire easily and flare up with a quick hot flame, thus setting fire to the branches, which are full of pitch and resin and burn freely.

No one but a grown person should light the candles. Children should be kept at a safe distance from the tree, doors and windows should be closed to exclude the draft, a constant watch should be kept while the candles are burning, and they should all be extinguished before a single present is taken from the tree. This is especially important if the presents are distributed by Santa Claus, as his long beard, and the cotton fur on his clothing, are easily ignited from the candles.

The celebration of the Fourth of July is one of the most

serious problems in the country. Fireworks are dangerous play-things and should be used with the greatest caution. Every year many persons are killed or injured, and valuable property is destroyed by the careless use of fireworks.

There are some kinds of fireworks which should never be used under any circumstances. Among these are cannon crackers, fire balloons, toy pistols, toy cannon, bombs, and revolvers firing blank cartridges.

On the day before the Fourth, all yards should be cleared of rubbish, as falling sparks might set it on fire. During the day of the celebration cellar windows should be closed, and stables and barns should be opened only when necessary.

In many cities the sale of dangerous fireworks is prohibited by law; but a common fire-cracker, a Roman candle, or a sky-rocket may cause serious damage if it is not handled properly.

THE SUNSHINE BAND

THE Sunshine Band was made up of twelve little girls, one for each of the twelve letters in their name. They wore badges of yellow ribbon just the color of sunshine, with the letters S. B. painted on them in white, and every time they had a meeting they sang their own special song; —

"Scatter sunshine all along your way,
Cheer and bless and brighten every passing day."

They had a secret, too, and a motto. Their motto was "Scatter Sunshine," and their secret—but I'm not going to tell you their secret. They didn't even tell me. I just guessed it.

They met every Saturday afternoon, first at one house and then another. Each little girl was always expected to tell a sunshine story, and if any one had disobeyed the rules of the club she had to pay a fine. Perhaps you will think that the rules were not so very hard to remember, but every once in a while a penny went clinking down to the bottom of their bank.

First of all they were expected to bring sunshine into their own homes. They must say "Good-morning" cheerfully, no matter if the day were cloudy and dismal. They must come to the table with clean hands and faces and a pleasant smile; and they must not frown or look cross if their mother asked them to wipe the dishes when they wanted to play out of doors.

Then all day long they must keep their eyes and ears open to find some helpful thing to do, no matter how small it might be; and if, at night, they had not done one tiny useful thing they must make a black cross against the day.

You would hardly believe how much sunshine they could make with very little trying, and how many pleasant tales they had to tell at their meetings.

Two of the girls gathered flowers every week for one of the hospitals; one did errands for a neighbor who was lame; three, who had sweet voices, gave little concerts at the home for aged women, and another read aloud to a blind girl every Monday afternoon after school.

Sometimes they packed boxes of old books and toys to send to a mission school in the South, and once they shook every penny out of their bank to buy fruit for a little sick girl.

Miss Hastings, who was the teacher of their class in Sunday-school, was also the leader of the band; and whenever they had an especially good sunshine story they carried it to her. She kept their badge of honor, too, unless some one was wearing it as a reward for good service.

In the largest cities the firemen find their hardest work

One Saturday afternoon, as soon as their meeting was over, they hurried off to her house. "Oh! Miss Hastings," they cried, when she opened the door, "Hilda Browning told the best story of all to-day, and we want her to have the badge right away."

"What is it, Hilda?" questioned Miss Hastings, after she had led the way to her sunny living-room.

"Tell her," urged all the other girls when Hilda hung back, her face rosy with blushes.

"It was nothing," said Hilda shyly, "I just happened to be there at the right time. That was all."

"Happened to be where?" asked the teacher, "and what do you mean by the right time?"

"At Mrs. Hazen's," said three or four of the girls at once. "The curtain caught fire from the gas jet and Hilda tore it down and threw it out of the window."

"Wait a minute!" begged their teacher, putting her hands over her ears; "I can't hear what you say when you all talk together. Now, Hilda, begin at the beginning."

So, with many promptings from the girls, who had heard the story from Mrs. Hazen herself, Hilda told how she had saved the house from fire.

"You know Mrs. Hazen has been sick with rheumatism for over a year," she said. "Her daughter, who has always taken care of her, has gone away for a two weeks' vacation, so I have been going there every afternoon after school to stay for an hour while the nurse takes a walk.

"Yesterday I said I would stay two hours because it was Friday and I didn't have any lessons to learn; and I took over my 'Youth's Companion' to read a story.

"It was such a cloudy afternoon that it grew dark while I was reading and Mrs. Hazen told me to light the gas. When I finished the story she asked me to open the bed-room window to let in some fresh air, and then bring her a glass of water.

"As I opened the kitchen door to get the water, a gust of wind blew the muslin window-curtain into the gas flame. It blazed up in an instant and Mrs. Hazen screamed for help."

"And when Hilda ran into the room and saw the curtain on fire she pulled it down with her bare hands and threw it out of the window," put in Ethel Strong. "The fingers on her right hand are all blistered, but she saved the house from catching fire."

"Perhaps she saved Mrs. Hazen's life, too," added Dorothy Hovey. "You know Mrs. Hazen has the rheumatism so badly that she cannot take a single step, and if she had been alone no one knows what might have happened."

"Now, Miss Hastings, don't you think Hilda deserves the badge of honor?" spoke up Alice Hunter.

"Yes, she certainly does," replied Miss Hastings, and, as she spoke, she took from its box a gold pin with the letters S. S. in blue enamel, and fastened it at Hilda's throat.

"Not all of us may ever have an opportunity to save a house from fire, or a life from danger," she added; "but if Hilda had not been doing a little kindness she would not have been ready in time of need to do a greater one."

Why did the girls call themselves the Sunshine Band?

What were some of their rules?

What did the letters S. S. mean on their badge of honor?

What kind things did they do?

How did the muslin curtain catch fire?

How could this have been prevented?

Why is it dangerous to have a gas jet near a window?

How should all gas flames be protected?

A gas jet should always be protected by a glass globe or a wire frame, and the bracket should be rigid so that it cannot be folded back against the wood-work, and cannot swing against curtains or draperies. If the curtain catches fire, pull it down quickly and smother the flames with a heavy rug. A woman should never attempt to stamp out the flames, as her skirts will easily catch fire.

If there is an odor of gas anywhere in the house, especially in a dark closet, do not search for the leak with a match or a lighted candle. If you should happen to find the leak you might cause an explosion or set the house on fire.

VACATION AT GRANDPA'S

DID I ever tell you about the time we boys set Grandpa Snow's barn on fire? It happened long ago, but I shall never forget it, if I live to be a hundred years old.

Kenneth and I always thought no better luck would ever come to us than to be told that we might spend the last week of July and the whole month of August with Grandpa and Grandma Snow.

Grandpa Snow owned a large farm up among the Green Mountains, and as our home was in the city, you can imagine how much it meant to us to hear that we were to spend five long weeks in the country.

I was eleven years old and Kenneth was eight, and as we had to change cars but once, Father said we might go all the way alone.

We left the station at eight o'clock in the morning, in the care of a good-natured, obliging conductor who promised to see that we changed cars safely at White River Junction, and the long ride in the train seemed just a part of the vacation fun.

I truly think that we did just as Mother would have liked us to do all that day. She looked so sweet and earnest when she bade us good-bye and said, "Now, boys, be kind and polite to everyone who speaks to you," that we couldn't help remembering her words.

There was a tired-looking woman on the train. She had a little boy who was tired, too, and he kept crying and fussing, until at last Kenneth said he was going to take him over in our seat and amuse him.

The boy was a jolly little fellow, about the age of our dear little baby sister at home, and we three had such a good time together that we could hardly believe our ears when the brakeman shouted out, "Walden! Walden!"

We gathered our bags and boxes together in a hurry, and bade good-bye to our new-found friends. In a minute we were out on the station platform, and the train was whizzing away without us; but we didn't have time to wonder if any one were coming to meet us, for down the road came Grandpa Snow, rattling along in a big hay-rack and waving his old straw hat at us.

"Hello, boys!" he said, as he pulled up his horses beside the platform; "we were pretty busy in the hay-field to-day, so I thought I could come right along, and give you a ride in my new hay-wagon. There's no fancy top on it, but there is plenty of room for both of you young chaps and all your baggage. You'll like it better than an automobile ride, I'll wager. So this is Leslie and Kenneth, is it? You surely have grown! Why, I can hardly tell one from the other, but I'll trust Grandma to know. She always seems to understand boys pretty well."

After a hug, and a hand-shake, and a hearty laugh, we jogged along up the road. Even if we were only boys I don't believe we shall ever forget that ride. It was late in the afternoon, and the air was so cool and sweet that it hardly seemed as if it could be the same hot, dusty day we began in the city. We could smell the cedar and fir-balsam all along the way, and every little while there was a bird-note like a sweet-toned bell.

It wasn't very long before we spied Grandpa's house, and dear old Grandma in the door waving her apron to us.

"Well, Mother," called out Grandpa, as we drove into the yard, "here are two new hired men for you. How do you think you will like them?"

By the way Grandma hugged us and kissed us, I guess she thought we would suit her pretty well. I remember something that suited us, too, and that was the good things we had to eat that night.

I wonder if there is any one else in the whole world who can cook like one's own grandmother? Perhaps there is, — but I know one thing, Grandma Snow was the best cook I ever saw. You should have seen that supper! There were hot biscuits, and fried chicken, and honey, and gingerbread, and cookies, and strawberry tarts, and cottage cheese, and so many good things that we couldn't eat half of them.

Every time we stopped eating Grandma would say, "Something must be the matter with these boys. They haven't any appetite." And Grandpa would look at us over his spectacles and answer, "They do look pale and thin. Give them another tart." Then he'd give one of his great laughs and shake all over like a big bowl of jelly.

We had just time after supper to help Grandpa and the hired man get in one load of hay. Then it was dark, and we were so tired and sleepy that we were glad to climb into bed, — just the highest, whitest, softest bed you ever saw.

We made Grandma promise to call us very early, and at five o'clock the next morning we were ready for breakfast and the day's work in the hay-field.

What fun it was to rake after the wagon, and to ride home on those great, sweet-smelling loads of hay!

Of course we had plenty of time to play, but we liked to work, too; and the work on a farm seems like play to boys who have always lived in the city.

We used to go down to the garden every morning to pick the vegetables for dinner, and we always helped Grandma shell the peas and string the beans. It took a good big panful, too, for we were pretty hungry up there on the farm.

Every morning we drove the cows to the pasture, and every afternoon we drove them home. We hunted for hens' eggs in the big barn, and went blueberrying and blackberrying. Kenneth made a collection of wild flowers, and Grandma showed him how to press them so that he could take them home.

What good times we did have! Even on rainy days there was always something to do, and we often had the most fun of all when it was raining the hardest. All the boys in the neighborhood got into the habit of coming to play with us in one of Grandpa's barns; and we used to have circuses and tight-rope walking and all sorts of games.

But one day, when we had been having a very jolly time together, one of the boys suggested that we should try a new game. "I'm tired of walking on beams and jumping off hay-mows," he said. "Let's do something different."

He took a whole bunch of matches out of his pocket and held them up. "Let's try scratching matches, and see who can scratch the most and blow them out again in one minute," he suggested.

I, for one, knew very well that matches were not made to play with, and I said so. Kenneth and Willie Smith agreed with me. So did Joe Wiggin and Peter Fisher, but four or five of the boys thought it would be great fun, and in spite of all we could say the match-race began.

Four boys sat down in a circle on the barn floor, lighting and blowing out the matches just as fast as they could, while Harry Plummer counted sixty.

In their hurry, they threw the matches down carelessly, and

before any of us noticed it, a lighted match had been thrown into the hay.

It blazed up in an instant, and before we could run to the field for help the whole barn was a roaring furnace. Joe Wiggin and Peter Fisher led out the two horses, and fortunately, the cows were in the pasture, for in less than half an hour the barn was burned to the ground. All the hay that we had worked so hard to get in was lost, besides some of Grandpa's tools and his new hay-rack.

Grandpa and the hired man got there in time to save the harnesses and a few little things, and then all we could do was just to stand there and watch the barn burn. The nearest fire-engine was in the village four miles away, and all the water we had was in one well.

Luckily Grandpa's buildings were not joined together, and as there was no wind, only that one barn was burned. But that was one too many.

I tell you, I shall never forget that fire, and to this day I can't see a boy with matches in his pocket without wanting to tell him this story and urge him to remember all his life that matches are made for use and not for playthings.

Tell of some of the good times you have had on a farm.

What did the boys do on rainy days?

What game did one of them propose?

What happened while they were playing this game?

What are matches made for?

How should they be used?

There are several kinds of matches,—brimstone matches, parlor matches, bird's-eye matches, and safety matches. Safety matches can be lighted only on their own box, and are, therefore, the safest match to use. Parlor matches, so called, are dangerous, as they break easily and the blazing head flies off, lodging in clothing, draperies, or furniture. The sale of parlor matches is forbidden by law in New York City on account of the great number of fires which have resulted from their use.

Common matches should be kept in a tin box; they should be used carefully, and never thrown away while they are burning, or even while the stick is still red-hot. It is a bad habit to have matches scattered around the house, or lying loose in bureau drawers, in desks, on tables, or in the pockets of clothing. There are many ways in which fires have been caused by loose matches. Lucifer or brimstone matches have been known to burst into flame from the heat caused by the sun's rays shining through a window pane.

THE FIRE DRILL

Iᴛ was a warm, sunny afternoon in October,—one of the days of Indian summer that come to tempt us out of doors after vacation is over, and work has begun in earnest.

The pupils of the sixth grade in the Ashland School looked longingly out of the windows as they put away their spellers and took the reading-books from their desks. Their teacher saw the look, and understood what it meant. When the hands of the clock pointed to half-past two, and the bell rang for a five-minutes' recess, she said, "You may put on your hats and coats, and we will spend a half-hour in our garden. I noticed this noon that it needed some attention."

The children looked at each other and nodded eagerly. It was just the day for a lesson in gardening, of that they felt sure, especially if it meant a whole half-hour out of doors.

The school garden was their greatest pleasure. They had spent many a happy hour working together over the flower beds, since that morning in April when Miss Brigham had ended their lesson in nature-study by asking, "How many would like to help me make a garden in the schoolyard?"

Every hand flew up instantly, every face brightened with delight. There was not a boy or girl in the room who was not eager to begin at once; and the moment the frost was well out of the ground they went to work.

The boys spaded up the soil, and the girls helped rake it over and mark it out in beds. There was a narrow strip the whole length of the fence for a hedge of sunflowers, and in front of it were three square plots, one for each of the three classes in the grade.

The children sent everywhere for seed catalogues, and

studied them eagerly. Each class bought its own seeds and planted them, and once every week they spent a half-hour hoeing, weeding, and watering the garden.

In one plot morning-glories climbed over a wire trellis and turned their bright faces to the morning sun, in another there was a gay riot of nasturtiums. During the summer the girls picked fragrant bouquets of sweet peas, and all through the fall they gathered sunny yellow marigolds for the teacher's desk.

But now Jack Frost had taken his turn at gardening. The nasturtiums and morning-glories hung in ragged festoons from their trellises, and the heavy heads of the sunflowers drooped from the top of the dry stalks. There was nothing left in the garden but a few hardy weeds that had grown in spite of the watchful gardeners.

"I don't see anything to do," said one of the girls, as she followed Miss Brigham across the schoolyard. "We may as well let the weeds grow now if they want to."

"We must clear everything away and get the garden ready for next spring," replied the teacher. "You can see for yourselves what ought to be done. I will stand here and watch you work."

After all there was plenty to do. One of the boys took out his knife and cut off the sunflower stalks, while the girls picked off the few seeds that the yellow-birds had left, and tied them up in a paper to save them for another year.

They tore down the vines, and pulled up the marigolds and zinnias. They straightened the trellises and smoothed over the empty beds. Then they picked up bits of paper that were blowing over the yard, and raked up the leaves that had fallen from the maple tree in the corner. When the work was finished there was a big pile of rubbish to be taken away.

"We might have a bonfire," suggested one of the boys.

"No," said Miss Brigham, "this west wind would blow all the smoke into the schoolhouse. Besides, there are too many houses near by. You can put the rubbish in the waste-barrels in the basement, and the janitor will take care of it."

The other children went back to the schoolroom, while the three largest boys were left to clean up the yard. The waste-barrels were full and running over; but they hunted around in the cellar and found an empty box in which they packed all the rubbish. Then they went upstairs and took up their work with the rest of the class.

Suddenly the big gong in the hall rang out sharply for the fire drill,—one, two, three! At the third stroke every book was closed, and in the sixteen rooms of the building all the pupils rose at once to their feet, ready to march down to the street. The doors were thrown wide open, and they passed out of their class-rooms in double file to meet another file from the opposite door, and move down the stairs four abreast, keeping step to the double-quick march played by one of the teachers.

On their way they passed the dressing-rooms, but no one took hat or cap from the hooks. There was not a moment to lose. Every child must be in the street in less than two minutes after the stroke of the third bell. They had done it over and over again, in exactly this same way, and the principal was standing at the door with his watch in his hand, counting off the seconds. He would know if a single child kept the line waiting.

"What a good day it is for a fire drill!" they thought, as they passed through the long halls and down the stairs; but before the last of the older pupils were out of the building they realized that this was no fire drill.

Smoke was already pouring through the cracks in the floor

and curling up around the registers. It filled the hall with a thick cloud that made them cough and choke as they marched through it; but not a boy pushed the boys in front of him, not a girl screamed or left her place, as the line moved steadily down the steps and across the yard to the street.

Two of the teachers stood at the gates to hurry the children off toward home, and even before the firemen came clattering around the corner, the big schoolhouse was empty and the pupils were safe.

After the fire was out and the excitement over, the fire chief and the principal sent for the boys who had taken the rubbish to the basement.

Yes, they had lighted some matches, they said, because the cellar was dark, the waste-barrels were all full, and they were trying to find an empty box. The head of one of the matches had broken off, but it was not burning, and they had not thought of it again.

It was possible that they might have stepped on it later and lighted it, and that the tiny flame had set fire to the waste paper on the floor.

"That was no doubt the cause of the fire," the fire chief agreed. "Parlor matches are often lighted in that same way. This was, of course, an accident; but even accidents can be avoided.

"In the first place there should never be any waste paper on the basement floor; and in the second place boys should never carry parlor matches, or any other kind of matches, to school. There are more precious lives in a schoolhouse than in any other building in the whole world."

Why was the rubbish put in the basement?

How did it catch fire?

How could this fire have been avoided?

Why is it dangerous to carry matches to school?

Why are parlor matches especially unsafe?

Have you ever seen a match break off when it was scratched?

What became of the head of the match?

Schoolhouses and public buildings should be provided with a metal-lined bin where waste paper and refuse may be temporarily collected, instead of allowing it to accumulate on the basement floor or in wooden boxes and barrels. This bin should be located away from the stairs or corridors, and should be so placed that water-pipes passing over it may be provided with sprinklers which would open automatically in case of fire.

There should be fire-escapes on the large buildings, and children should be taught how to use them. All doors should open outward, and should never be locked during the school sessions. Fire drills should be practiced regularly, and every child in the building should understand the necessity for marching out promptly and in order.

Chemical fire-extinguishers, or pails well filled with water and marked "For Fire Only," should be set in conspicuous places on each floor near the stair-landings, and in the basements.

FIGHTING THE FIRE

EVERY village, town, and city is liable at any moment to have a fire. If this fire gets well under way it may become a conflagration, which no single fire department can control. For this reason promptness in reaching the fire with suitable apparatus is of the very first importance.

Great responsibility rests upon the firemen. They must be cool-headed, but quick in action; cautious, but daring; ready in an instant to perform difficult and dangerous tasks, often at the risk of their own lives. Every great fire makes heroes. It is this life of excitement and daring that attracts men and makes them eager to fight the great battles against fire.

In olden times methods of fighting fire were very simple. The only apparatus consisted of axes, buckets, ropes, and short ladders. Men and boys ran to the fire and did their best to put out the flames, but they had no leader and could not work to advantage.

The first fire-engines were drawn through the streets by men, instead of horses, and water was forced through the hose by means of a hand-pump worked by these same men.

Every year the system of fire protection is being perfected, new apparatus is invented, and better methods are introduced.

In the smaller towns the fire companies consist largely of volunteer firemen, who leave their work at the sound of the alarm and hurry to the scene of action. But in the larger cities the fire-department is like a well-organized army, with its chiefs, captains, lieutenants, and privates, always prepared to wage a never-ending war against the fires.

Most of these men live in the engine-houses, and are ready at any moment, day or night, to answer an alarm. The horses stand free in their stalls, awaiting the signal, trained like the men to instant action.

With the first stroke of the great gong the horses leave their stalls and stand beside the pole of the engine. The harness, suspended in mid-air, falls upon their backs, and almost before the men can jump up and cling to their places on the engine, the driver picks up the reins, the horses plunge through the open door and gallop madly down the street.

The driver leans out over the pole, his hands far apart, holding the reins in an iron grasp and guiding the flying horses safely along the winding way.

Gongs clang, whistles blow, bells ring! The streets are cleared as if by magic. Heavy teams are drawn up beside the curbing; electric cars stand still; men, women, and children hurry to the sidewalks, or stand in open doorways waiting for the engines to go tearing along to the fire. The fire apparatus has the right of way!

When the scene of the fire is reached, the driver pulls up the horses so quickly that they are almost thrown on their haunches; the engine is wheeled into place beside the hydrant, the hose is attached and straightened out along the street.

The police have already drawn a fire-line, and are driving back the eager, curious crowd; but the firemen have eyes or ears for nothing but the fire. The chief shouts his orders and they hasten to obey. The horses are led away to a place of safety, and ladders are brought up to be used in case of need.

The water-tower pours a stream into the upper windows

Two or three men seize the nozzle of the great hose and

rush with it into the burning building to seek the heart of the fire. Smoke pours from the doors and windows in dense clouds, blinding and choking them until they gasp for breath. Water slops and spatters everywhere, steam rises from the blazing timbers, and the intense heat scorches and stifles them as they work.

At last the smoke clears away, the water is shut off, and then, with picks and axes, the firemen search under fallen timbers lest some tiny blaze may still be smouldering in a hidden corner.

At a quick order from the chief, the hose is rapidly drawn back and folded in its place, the horses are harnessed again to the engine, and the men return to the engine-house, to await their next call to action.

In the largest cities, which have grown rapidly skyward, piling one story on top of another in office buildings and dwelling houses, the firemen find their hardest work. This is especially true in the crowded tenement districts, where hundreds of people live under a single roof.

Here men, women, and children have to be rescued from upper windows and roofs, by means of scaling-ladders and life-lines; and sometimes they even have to drop into life-nets which the firemen hold to catch them.

If the building is so high that the water from the hose cannot reach the flames, the water-tower is brought to the scene of action, and a stream is poured into the building through windows many stories above the ground.

In every large fire-department several different kinds of apparatus are needed. There is a chemical engine for use in case the fire proves to be small and easily controlled. There are long trucks loaded with ladders, tools, and ropes; and there are also the regular fire engines, sometimes drawn by plunging horses, sometimes driven through the streets at a high rate of speed by a powerful motor. These motors are superior to horses because they can reach the fire more quickly, and can carry heavier and more powerful engines.

In the harbors, and in some of the larger rivers and lakes, there are fire-boats to be used in case of fire along the water-front, or in vessels at the docks. These boats always have plenty of water at hand, and often do valuable work in saving property on the wharfs and piers.

VERNON'S BROTHER

IF any one had asked Vernon Houston what he wanted more than anything in the whole world, he would not have waited an instant before replying, "A brother!"

He had pets of all kinds,—rabbits, guinea pigs, a dog, and a pony; but still his lonely little heart longed for a brother, some one to enjoy all his pleasures, some one to go to school with, some one to play with when his father and mother were away and only Jane was left in the kitchen.

To be sure he had books and games without number, but he soon grew tired of reading, and what good were games when there was no one to play with him?

Of course he had plenty of school friends and playmates, but on stormy days, or when he and Jane were left all alone, there were never any boys to be found,—just when he most needed them.

In spite of his dog and his pony and all his rabbits he couldn't help being a little lonely. Whenever he saw two brothers playing together, he always thought how glad he would be to exchange every one of his pets—pony and all— for a little brother, and every Christmas he wrote a letter to Santa Claus to ask for one.

On his ninth birthday his father and mother surprised him by saying that they were going to Boston. They promised to come home the next day and bring him the best birthday gift he ever had in all his life; but what this delightful gift was to be they would not tell. It was a secret, and a very good secret, too.

To tell the truth Mr. and Mrs. Houston had decided to adopt a little boy. They had been planning it for some time, but

Vernon knew nothing about it. They had always been sorry for their brotherless son, and they knew how many boys there are in the world who have no home, no father and mother, no one to love them and care for them.

They had been waiting to hear of some homeless lad, who was good and honest, to take into their home and hearts, and to become the "little brother" for whom Vernon longed. At last a man telephoned from Boston that he had found just the boy they wanted, so they set off at once to bring home the birthday gift.

When they looked into Harry's bright eyes and honest face, they were not long in deciding that he was just the right boy for them.

Mrs. Houston bent and kissed him, and Mr. Houston took him by the hand, saying kindly, "Harry, how would you like to come and live with us, to be our boy, and a brother to our son, Vernon?"

Harry was too happy to say a word, but his big brown eyes answered for him, and it was not long before they were all three on their way to Greenfield.

I wish you could have seen Vernon when his father and mother arrived with the birthday gift.

"Here, my boy, is the secret,—the brother you have been waiting for so long," said Mr. Houston. "Let me introduce you to your new brother Harry. He has come to stay as long as he can be happy with you. He is only a few months younger than you are, and I don't see why you two boys can't have a good time together."

It seemed as if the boys had only to look straight into each other's eyes to become the best of friends, and if you could have watched them as the days went by, you would have thought they were as happy as children could possibly be.

Vernon brought out all his playthings and gave half of them to Harry; he showed him how to make Rags do all sorts of funny tricks; he let him feed the rabbits and the guinea-pigs; and when they went to ride, he let Harry drive the pony. How the little fellow did enjoy holding the reins and riding in a red pony-cart like those he had looked at so many times before with longing eyes.

The two boys ran races, played ball, and went to school together. Vernon never complained of being lonely, and as for Harry, he was the happiest boy you ever saw. He tried to show how grateful he was for everything that Mr. and Mrs. Houston did for him; and he resolved to study hard, to be honest and true, and never to forget to do all in his power to repay his kind friends.

The brothers had a room together with two white beds standing side by side. One night Mr. Houston came home very late and found that the boys had gone to bed, so he went to their room to bid them good-night.

He was much surprised to find both the boys reading a book, with a lighted lamp on a little stand between their beds.

"My sons," he said very seriously, "I always like to see you enjoying your books, but I cannot allow you to read after you are in bed."

"Why not, Father?" questioned Vernon.

"Because it is a dangerous thing to do," Mr. Houston replied. "You might fall asleep without blowing out the light. It is a common thing to have such an accident. Lamps are often tipped over and houses set on fire in just that way."

"But, Father," urged Vernon, "please let us finish this chapter. It will take only a few minutes longer, and it is such a good story."

"You may finish this one chapter," Mr. Houston answered. "Then you must blow out the light, and after to-night there must be no more reading in bed with a lighted lamp."

The boys meant to obey their father; but they were both very sleepy, and before the end of the chapter was reached, they were sound asleep.

It was not long before Vernon restlessly threw out his arm. His hand hit the lamp and knocked it off the table, and the oil spread over the carpet, taking fire from the burning wick.

Rags had crept into the room to sleep on his little master's bed, and the noise waked him. When he saw the blazing oil, he jumped down and ran out into the hall, barking with all his might.

Mr. and Mrs. Houston rushed upstairs and beat out the flames with heavy rugs, before the bed clothing caught fire; but the boys were terribly frightened, and no one ever had to tell them again not to read in bed with a lighted lamp. They had learned a good lesson, and little Rags had become a never-to-be-forgotten hero.

Why was Vernon lonely?

What gift did he have on his ninth birthday?

Why did the boys set a lighted lamp on the table beside their bed?

How was it overturned?

Where was Rags? What did he do?

How should this fire have been avoided?

A lamp, a lantern, or an oil-stove should not be placed where it could possibly be upset. Neither should it be blown out until the wick has been turned half-way down, as the flame might be blown into the oil, thus causing an explosion. To turn down the wick too low, however, is also dangerous.

All brass or metal work on a lamp or oil-stove should be kept clean and bright, as dirty metal retains the heat, thus causing vapor to rise from the oil, and making an explosion possible.

THE WORLD'S GREAT FIRES

EVER since men have built their houses of wood, and have crowded their dwellings together in cities, there have been terrible conflagrations, destroying, in two or three days, property which has been gathered together at a great cost of time and labor. Thousands of people have been made homeless, and fortunes have been lost in a single night.

As long ago as 65 A. D., when Nero was Emperor of Rome, more than half the city was destroyed by a great fire, and the people were obliged to flee to the hills for safety.

Constantinople has suffered eleven conflagrations, by which more than 130,000 homes have been destroyed; and in Japan, where the houses are built of bamboo and paper, fires sweep through the streets with the rapidity of the wind, burning hundreds of the little low buildings in a single hour. In fact, these fires are of such common occurrence, and are so destructive, that the Japanese people keep their valuable possessions in fireproof storehouses in their own gardens, and they often have the frame and paper walls of a new house in this "godown," ready to put together as soon as the ashes of their former dwelling are cool enough not to set another fire.

In September, 1666, the city of London was devastated by flames. The fire broke out in a baker's shop, and spread on all sides so rapidly that it could not be extinguished before two-thirds of the city had been destroyed. All the sky was illuminated by the flames, and the light could be seen for forty miles. More than a thousand houses were in flames at the same time. Night was as light as day, and the air was so hot that the people could do nothing but stand still and look on at their own ruin.

In those days there was little fire-fighting apparatus, nothing at all to be compared with our modern conveniences; and the flames, fanned by a strong east wind, swept through the narrow streets, fairly eating up the houses, which were built entirely of wood. The ruins covered 436 acres; 400 streets were laid waste, 13,200 houses were destroyed, and 200,000 persons were made homeless.

The first of the great conflagrations in our own country was the fire in Chicago in October, 1871. This fire was caused by a cow kicking over a lighted lantern in a barn; and, from this simple start, three and one-half square miles were laid waste, 200 persons were killed, 17,450 buildings were destroyed, and 98,500 persons were made homeless. The flames were fanned by a fierce gale, and spread with great rapidity, raging uncontrolled for two days and nights.

In November, 1872, the city of Boston was visited by fire. The conflagration was confined almost wholly to the business district, and while only 800 buildings were destroyed, the loss amounted to $73,000,000, and hundreds of men lost their entire fortune.

In April, 1906, San Francisco was devastated by the most terrible fire known to all history. The fire was preceded by earthquake shocks, and, with the falling walls and chimneys, fires were started in different sections of the city. The earthquake also caused the bursting of the water mains in the streets, so that it was impossible to hold the flames in check; and before they were at last extinguished the burned area was over three times greater than that of the Chicago fire, and ten times that of the Boston fire. This fire destroyed $350,000,000 worth of property, and over 300,000 persons were made homeless.

The Baltimore fire, in 1904, burned over 140 acres, and $85,000,000 worth of property was lost.

This great waste is a serious problem which confronts our country; but each one of us, by being careful, may do his share toward lessening the loss by fire.

NEW YEAR'S EVE

IT was the last night of the year, and a happy little group was sitting around the supper table in the Hawleys' pleasant dining-room.

There were Mr. and Mrs. Hawley and their two children, — Leland, who was a wide-awake boy of fourteen, and Rachel, who was two years younger. Their cousins, Lawrence and Dorothy, had come to spend several weeks with them. As they were all about the same age, the four children were having a merry time together.

The Hawley homestead was in a little country town in New England; but Lawrence and Dorothy had always lived in the city of New Orleans and they knew nothing about winter and winter sports. You can imagine how much they enjoyed everything, especially the snow.

They were all laughing and chatting merrily when suddenly Mr. Hawley rose and went to the window. "I hear sleigh-bells," he said. "A sleigh is driving into our yard."

In a moment more a knock was heard at the door, and a note was handed to Mrs. Hawley telling her that her sister was very ill.

This sister lived several miles away, but Mrs. Hawley felt that she must go to her at once, so her husband decided to harness his pair of bays and drive her over.

"I am sorry to leave you, children," Mrs. Hawley said, as she tied on her bonnet. "Have just as good a time as you can, and I will trust you not to do anything that would displease me."

"I will take Mother over and return as soon as possible,"

said Mr. Hawley, as he tucked his wife into the sleigh. "I shall try to be home before ten o'clock; but don't sit up for me. Be good children and take care of everything."

"Perhaps my sister will be better and I can come home to-morrow," added Mrs. Hawley cheerfully. Then she kissed the children and bade them good-bye, and the horses dashed off down the road with a great jingling of bells.

The girls looked a little sober when they went back into the big empty farmhouse, but Leland tried to cheer them up. "We'll have a jolly time keeping house," he said. "What's the first thing to be done?"

"The dishes, of course," replied his sister; "there are always dishes to do, no matter what happens."

The boys cleared the table, while Rachel and Dorothy washed and wiped the dishes, and set the table for breakfast. Then they brought in some wood and built a big fire in the fireplace.

The flames went roaring up the chimney, and the children sat for a long time before the fire, watching the rings of sparks that twisted in and out on the soot-covered bricks. "Children going home from school," they called them, and the last one to burn out was the one to stay after school for a whipping.

"Let's roast some chestnuts," Leland suggested, when there was a good bed of hot ashes, and he ran up in the attic to get a bagful that he had been saving for just such an occasion.

It was fun to push the chestnuts into the fire with a long poker and then watch them pop out when they were roasted. Sometimes they flew across the room, or under the tables and chairs, and then there was a great hunt for them.

"We might wish on the chestnuts," Rachel suggested. "If

they pop out on the hearth, our wish will come true, but if they fly into the fire, it won't."

"Oh, yes!" cried Lawrence; "that's just the thing to do. Girls first, — you begin, Rachel."

"No, Dorothy is my guest," replied his cousin; "she must have the first turn."

Dorothy poked her chestnut into the ashes. "I wish I might spend the whole year up here with you," she said; and when the nut popped right into her lap the other children joined hands and danced around her in a circle.

Then it was Rachel's turn, and she wished for higher marks in school than she ever had before; but the chestnut jumped into the fire and blazed up merrily.

"That's because your marks are good enough anyway," her brother told her. "What is your wish, Lawrence?"

"I wish that I might go to London in an airship," Lawrence replied.

"And I wish that I might go to the biggest circus in the world," added Leland, poking his chestnut in beside his cousin's.

One of the nuts popped into the farthest corner of the hearth, and the other burned to a little black cinder; but the boys couldn't decide whose chestnut it was that flew away, so they couldn't tell which one was to have his wish.

"I'll tell you something that is just as good as flying," said Leland. "Let's get out our bob-sled and go coasting. There's a moon to-night, and it is almost as light as day."

"I don't think we ought to leave the house," objected Rachel. "Father and Mother are both away, you know, and they told us to be careful."

"Oh, don't be a goose!" her brother replied. "The house can

take care of itself."

"We ought to put out all the lamps then, and cover the fire with ashes," said thoughtful Rachel.

"Nonsense!" exclaimed Leland. "We won't be gone long. The fire is all right. There is nothing left but the back-log, and that will not burn much longer."

"I'm going to put out the lamps any way," said his sister. "I feel sure that Mother never leaves them lighted when there is no one in the house."

"Well, hurry up then," urged Leland. "You girls bundle up well, and Lawrence and I will get out the sled."

In a few minutes the boys came running up to the door with the sled, and as soon as the girls were well tucked in, they took hold of the rope and pranced off like wild horses.

There was a full moon, and they could see the road perfectly. The air was crisp and clear, and the snow shone and sparkled like diamonds.

"It seems like a winter fairyland," said Dorothy. "Let's keep watch for the fairies. They ought to come trooping across the fields dressed in pretty white furs, and dance under the trees to the music of sleigh-bells."

The sled seemed to fairly fly over the snow, and when they came to the top of the long hill, the boys jumped on and they all went coasting down, with shouts of laughter.

Up and down, up and down they went; and such fun as they did have! Of course they stayed out much longer than they meant to; but at last Rachel said, "It must be getting late. Father was coming home at ten, and he will wonder what has become of us."

The boys trotted home again more slowly, and as they came in sight of the house they saw that Mr. Hawley had already arrived before them. The rooms downstairs were brightly lighted, and when they passed the living-room windows they saw him hurrying to and fro as if he were busy about some work.

"Here we are, Father," called Leland. "We've been out coasting."

"And we've had such a good time!" added Dorothy. Then, as she entered the living-room, she exclaimed in amazement: "What is the matter, Uncle Henry? What have you been doing in here?"

Her uncle crossed the room and opened the windows. Then he took off his hat and overcoat, and wiped great beads of perspiration from his face, while the children stood in the doorway looking around at the disordered room.

"When I came home the house was on fire," he answered, "and I've had a pretty busy time for the last ten minutes. You children must have left a log burning on the hearth, and a spark flew out and set the rug on fire. Then the table and one of the chairs caught fire from the rug, and if I hadn't come home just when I did, we might not have had any home by this time."

"It was my fault, Father," spoke up Leland. "Rachel wanted to bury the log in the ashes; but I told her it wouldn't do any harm to leave it burning."

"I suppose it was partly my fault, too," said Mr. Hawley. "I've always intended to buy a wire screen for this fireplace. It is never safe to go out of the room and leave an open fire. When we go to town to-morrow to buy a new rug, we will buy a screen and a fender, too."

"And the next time we light a fire on the hearth," added Lawrence, "we'll stay at home and take care of it, even if it is a moonlight night and we do want to go coasting."

Why did Lawrence and Dorothy enjoy the New England winter?

What did the children do after Mr. and Mrs. Hawley went away?

Why did Rachel put out the lights before leaving the house?

What accident happened as a result of leaving a burning log in the fireplace?

How could this accident have been prevented?

It is never safe to have an open fire in a fireplace unless it is protected with a wire screen. Sparks often fly from the burning wood and set fire to rugs, draperies, and clothing, or sometimes a blazing log rolls out on to the floor.

If it is necessary to leave the fire before it is entirely burned out, the logs may be taken from the andirons and buried in the ashes. This should always be done before the fire is left for the night, as a change of wind might cause a smouldering log to become a dangerous firebrand.

CHRISTMAS CANDLES

IT was Christmas Eve,—the happiest, merriest time in all the year,—and no one need look at a calendar to know it. The shop windows were full of gifts and toys of every description, and in some of the larger shops jolly old Santa Claus himself was waiting to shake hands with the boys, or pat the curly heads of the little girls.

Crowds of people were hurrying to and fro on the streets, their arms filled with packages of all shapes and sizes. Here was a man carrying a doll carriage, and a woman with a tiny wheelbarrow. There was a girl with a pair of snowshoes, and a boy with a Christmas-tree over his shoulder; but no matter how heavy were the bundles, or how crowded the streets, everyone seemed happy, and "Merry Christmas!" "Merry Christmas to you!" was heard on every side in friendly greeting.

Just enough snow had fallen to bring out the sleighs, and the jingling sleigh-bells added their merry music to the Christmas gayety. The air was clear and crisp, and beyond the city streets, with their glare of electricity, the stars shone with a clear light, just as the Star of the East shone so many centuries ago upon the little Babe of Bethlehem.

Yes, Christmas was everywhere. It shone from the stars, and from the happy faces of the children; and it made the whole world glad with the gladness of giving.

In the little town of Lindale, just as in all the other towns and cities, there was the greatest excitement. The houses were brightly lighted, people were hurrying to and fro in the streets, doors were carefully opened and closed, stockings were hung beside the chimneys, and Christmas trees were decorated with tinsel and candles and loaded with gifts for young and old.

But in the big brick church in the center of the town was the best Christmas tree of all. It stood on the floor and held its head up to the very ceiling, where a star gleamed with a golden light like the brightest star in the sky.

The branches were covered with frost that sparkled like diamonds, and under the trees were heaped big snowbanks of white cotton. Ropes of tinsel and strings of popcorn were twined in and out in long festoons, and tiny Christmas candles were set everywhere among the branches. Big dolls and little dolls peeped out through the green leaves, and here and there were Teddy bears, white rabbits, curly-haired puppies, woolly lambs, parrots on their perches, and canaries in tiny cages, — all toys, of course, but toys so wonderfully made that they looked as if they were really and truly alive.

Fire Drill for the Firemen

Piled high on the banks of snow were the Christmas gifts, big packages and little ones, all in white paper tied with red and green ribbons; and when the candles were lighted the whole tree looked as if it had been brought from fairyland and set down here to make the children happy.

This tree, with all its gifts and decorations, had been arranged by the pupils and teachers of the Sunday-school for the little children of the Lindale Mission.

For two or three months these "Willing Helpers," as they called themselves, had devoted all their spare minutes to getting everything ready. They had contributed toys and games, they had earned the money for some of the gifts, they had brought tinsel and gilded nuts from home, they had strung the popcorn, and, best of all, they had spent two happy evenings decorating the tree and tying up the packages.

Now, at last, it was Christmas Eve. At seven o'clock the church bells began to peal out their merriest welcome, and from all the houses came boys and girls with their fathers and mothers, eager to enjoy the pleasure of making others happy.

The little children of the Mission school were gathered in the chapel, and when everything was ready the doors were thrown wide open and they came marching in to see the tree.

As they moved slowly up the long aisle toward their seats in the front of the church, they sang a Christmas carol, keeping time with their marching; and their childish voices made the very rafters ring with joy.

The church bells pealed out once more, and a little boy at the head of the procession jingled some sleigh-bells, while every one joined in the chorus of the song: —

"Merry, merry, merry, merry Christmas bells,
Oh! sweetly, sweetly, chime;
Let your happy voices on the breezes swell,
This merry, merry Christmas time."

The Sunday-school pupils answered with another carol,

and the superintendent made a little speech of welcome. Then, when the children were all on tiptoe with excitement, there was a loud jangling of bells in the street, a stamping of feet at the door, and in came Santa Claus himself, with his great fur coat, his long white beard, and a heavy pack on his back.

Behind him came six pages, dressed in red and white, with little packs on their backs. They ran up and down the aisles, giving bags of candy to the children, and all the while the Christmas candles burned lower and lower, the tiny flames danced and flickered, the hat wax melted and dripped from bough to bough.

At last the superintendent of the Sunday-school began giving out the presents, and some of the teachers went to help him. Santa Claus himself called out the names, and the children ran up to receive their gifts from his hands.

In the midst of all this joy and happiness everyone forgot the lighted candles, until suddenly some one screamed, "Fire, fire! The tree is on fire!"

Then what a commotion there was! Men ran forward to put out the blaze, but it was so high up that no one could reach it. Two or three boys hurried down to the cellar for the step-ladder, several men ran to get pails of water, women snatched up their little children and took them into the street, hatless and coatless, while the teachers gathered up the few remaining gifts and tried to calm their frightened pupils.

In less time than it takes to tell it, the boys came rushing upstairs with a step-ladder, men came back with buckets of water, and Santa Claus climbed up to put out the fire which was running swiftly from one branch to another. In his hurry he knocked off another candle, it dropped into the white cotton and set the snowbanks blazing; but there were plenty of men to put out the flames before they could do any damage.

When the fire was all out, and the children had gone home, and were tucked safely in their little beds, the tree was left standing alone in the dark church. But it no longer looked as if it had come from fairyland. All the upper branches were burned off, wet strings of tinsel and popcorn drooped from the ends of the boughs, the gold star was black with smoke, and the snowbanks seemed to have suffered from a January thaw.

The next morning some of the fathers and mothers came to clear away the remains of the festivity and its disaster, and the children came to help them. "We'll never have another Christmas-tree as long as we live," declared one of the older girls. "Oh, yes, we will," her brother told her. "We'll have one next year for the Mission children; but we shall know better than to have it lighted with candles."

"Or, if we do use candles," added one of the teachers, "we'll have six boys to watch them every minute, and we will put out every one before we distribute a single gift."

"That's right," said a voice that sounded very much like that of Santa Claus; "this fire has taught us a good lesson, but it came very near spoiling all our happiness. No one can be too careful of fire where there are so many little children. One child's life is worth more than all the Christmas candles in the world."

What is the happiest day of the year for children?

When is Christmas Day?

What do you do on Christmas Eve?

Have you ever had a Christmas tree?

How was it decorated?

Why is it dangerous to light it with candles?

Why is it dangerous to use cotton to represent frost and snow?

How was this fire caused?

How could it have been avoided?

Christmas candles cause many fires. A Christmas tree should be fastened firmly so that it cannot be upset. It should not be decorated with paper, cotton, or any other inflammable material. Cotton should not be used to represent frost or snow, as it catches fire easily. If the snow effect is desired, asbestos or mineral wool can be used with safety.

The candles should be set upright in the holders, and should be placed so that they cannot set fire to the branches above. They should never be lighted by children. They should be watched constantly, and should be extinguished before the gifts are distributed, as they sometimes set fire to clothing. This more frequently happens if the person who distributes the gifts is dressed as Santa Claus, as his long beard and the cotton fun on his red coat and cap are especially inflammable.

Electricity is a safer method of lighting a Christmas tree. Wiring is now especially prepared which can be easily applied to the tree, and connected to the chandelier like an ordinary electric lamp. Bulbs in the shapes of birds, animals, clowns, etc., make the tree very attractive.

WHAT TO DO IN CASE OF FIRE

IN case of fire it is necessary above all things to *"keep cool."* Try not to get excited, and so waste precious moments in running about to no purpose. Act quickly, but keep your mind on what you are doing.

If it is only a little blaze, throw water on the thing that is burning, try to smother the flames with a heavy rug, or beat them out with a wet broom. If oil is burning, never pour on water, as this only spreads the oil and makes matters worse. For an oil fire use sand, earth from flower-pots, or big panfuls of flour.

If the fire is well started and you see at once that you cannot put it out alone, call for help by shouting "Fire!" at the door or window where some one will be likely to hear you.

Then summon the fire department. The best way to do this is to run to the nearest fire-alarm box, break the glass which will release the key, then unlock the door and pull down the hook. This rings the alarm at the engine-house. Everyone should know the location of the nearest box, and the way to ring the alarm.

If you can send some one else to ring the alarm, telephone to the nearest fire station. The number of this station should always hang in a conspicuous place near your telephone. If there is no fire alarm system, and you have no telephone, shout "Fire!" and arouse the neighbors.

If you leave the house to summon help, be sure to *close the door.* Fresh air will make the flames burn faster, and spread more rapidly. If the fire is in one room, try to keep it there by closing the doors and windows. If it is in a closet, shut the door until you can get help. In this way you may save the whole house from burning.

After you have given the alarm try to save what you can. Valuable papers should be taken care of first; then jewelry, silverware, heirlooms, and anything you especially treasure. Think about what you are doing. *Don't waste time* trying to save a looking-glass or clock, when you might put a handful of expensive silverware in your pocket.

If you are awakened in the night by the smell of smoke or the crackling of fire, do not stop to dress. Wrap yourself in a blanket or quilt, and waken everyone in the house, remembering especially little children and sick or aged people.

Then, after you have called the fire department, find out where the fire is and what it is best to do. If the fire is on the lower floor, do not go upstairs, as you might be unable to come down again. If the halls are filled with smoke, you can pass through them more easily by crawling on your hands and knees, for the smoke and hot air rise toward the ceiling, and the air is cooler and purer near the floor.

If it is necessary for you to go into a room that is filled with dense smoke, tie a wet towel or sponge over your nose and mouth. If you have no time to do this, hold a heavy woollen cloth over the lower part of your face, or, at least, turn up your coat collar.

If the lower part of the house is on fire, and you cannot go down the stairs, prepare to escape through the window, but *do not jump out* recklessly. First of all, close the door to keep out the fire and smoke as long as possible. Then drop the mattresses and pillows to the ground so that they will form a break in case you should fall. If possible tie the sheets and blankets firmly together to make a rope. Fasten it securely to the bed-post, after you have drawn the bed close to the window, and then, when it is absolutely necessary, let yourself down, hand over hand. This is a dangerous method of escape, and should only be used as a last resort. Try to wait for the firemen to rescue you.

If you see a fire anywhere, no matter how small, it is always best to give it immediate attention. If it is only a burning match or cigarette stump, step on it. If it is a fire in leaves, grass, or brush, put it out yourself or call for help. If it is in a house, notify the occupants at once, as they may not know anything about it. If the house is unoccupied, or the family is away from home, call the fire department. If a barn or stable is on fire, the first thing to do is to save the live stock.

After the fire is all out, the next care should be to protect the house and its contents from further damage by fire or theft, and to carry articles which have been taken out to a place of safety.

FIRST AID

I𝐹 a person's clothing is on fire, he should neither run nor scream, as running fans the flames, and screaming causes deep breathing, thereby drawing the intense heat into the lungs.

To extinguish the flames wrap the person tightly in a rug, blanket, or heavy woollen coat, and roll him upon the floor. This method is much more effective than using water. Often a person whose clothing is on fire will resist any efforts to aid him, owing to his intense fright.

When the flesh is burned or scalded, the first object of treatment is to relieve the pain.

Fire raging through the deserted streets in San Francisco

This is best accomplished by excluding all air from contact with the injured surface, either by dredging the part thickly with flour, if the skin is not broken, or by applying bandages. The best bandages are made of lint, cotton, or soft cloths moistened with water, or, better still, with water to which a little baking-soda has been added.

Be especially careful to remove all clothing covering a burn with the utmost care. Never try to pull it off. Cut it away, a tiny piece at a time, if necessary, so that the skin may not be broken and thus cause a more serious wound. Never hold a burn in front of the fire, as this only makes matters worse. As soon as the clothing has been removed apply the bandages, and if the burn is at all serious send for a physician.

If the person receives serious burns, he may become faint or lose consciousness from the effect of the shock to the nervous system. If this occurs, lay him flat on the floor or couch; preserve all body heat by covering him with warm clothing; apply cool applications to his head and heat to his feet.

ARTIFICIAL RESPIRATION

IF a person is overcome by inhaling smoke, it may be necessary to resort to artificial respiration. This is done as follows:

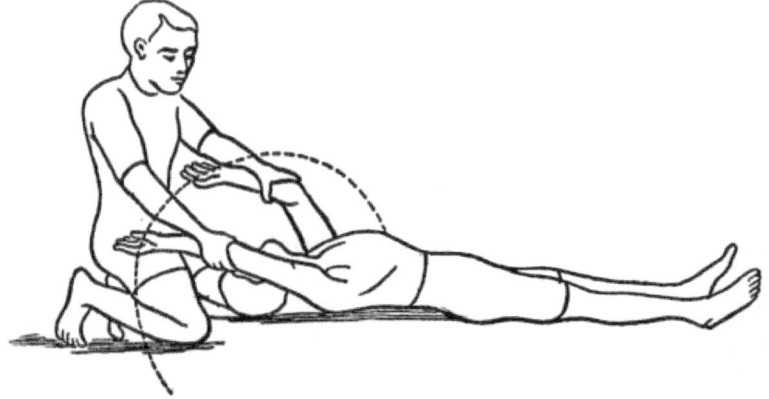

FIG. 1.

Lay the person to be treated flat on his back. Then kneel behind his head, grasp both arms near the elbow, and move them horizontally, carrying them away from the body and describing a semicircle until the hands meet above the head, as in Fig. 1. When this position has been reached, give the arms a steady pull for two seconds. By doing this the lungs are filled with air, because the ribs are drawn upward, thereby increasing the capacity of the chest.

The next step is to return the arms to the first position alongside the chest, as in Fig. 2, making considerable pressure against the lower ribs, and thereby forcing the impure air out of the lungs.

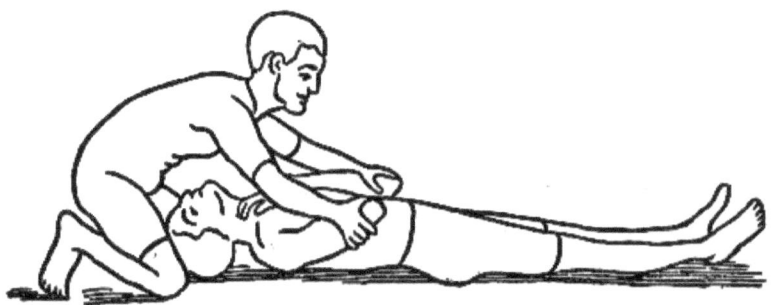

FIG. 2.

This whole act should occupy three or four seconds and be repeated sixteen times per minute. Do not abandon this work until it is definitely certain that the heart has ceased to beat.

www.ingramcontent.com/pod-product-compliance
Lightning Source LLC
Chambersburg PA
CBHW032001010726
47493CB00007B/2279